Woo! Hoo!

# EAT THE DARK

DEL
REY

BALLANTINE BOOKS
NEW YORK

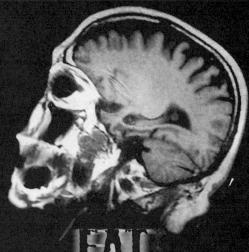

# EAT
# THE
# DARK

A NOVEL

## JOE SCHREIBER

SCHRE

A Del Rey Trade Paperback Original

Copyright © 2007 by Joe Schreiber

Published in the United States by Del Rey Books, an imprint of The Random House Publishing Group, a division of Random House, Inc., New York.

DEL REY is a registered trademark and the Del Rey colophon is a trademark of Random House, Inc.

LIBRARY OF CONGRESS CATALOGING-IN-PUBLICATION DATA
Schreiber, Joe.
Eat the dark : a novel / Joe Schreiber.
p.    cm.
ISBN 978-0-345-48750-6 (pbk. : acid-free paper)
1. Serial murderers—Fiction.    I. Title.
PS3619.C4635E28  2007
813'.6—dc22    2007022352

Printed in the United States of America

www.delrey.com

9 8 7 6 5 4 3 2 1

FIRST EDITION

Book design by Simon M. Sullivan

For Jack and Veda,

"Let me tell you a story…"

# ACKNOWLEDGMENTS

Once again I find myself deeply indebted to my agent, Phyllis Westberg, and my editor, Keith Clayton, for their persistence, diligence, and general midwifery along this lengthy road. It's not hyperbole: I couldn't have done it without them.

I owe a long overdue salute to my parents, Paul Schreiber and Kathy Peerbolte, for always believing in me and encouraging me for as long as I can remember.

Mad props to Martin "Mr. Wiggles" Sweeney for providing the fully loaded iPod during the last revision process, when I needed it most.

Thank you again, Christina and kids, for giving me the time and space to keep writing.

Finally, I am grateful to the staff and all my coworkers at Penn State Milton S. Hershey Medical Center, in particular George Stoltz, for a memorable tour through the underground tunnels and lesser-known passageways of that facility.

The hospital within these pages is a work of fiction.

EAT THE DARK

Mike Hughes thought: *It's dead.*

From where he stood, Tanglewood Memorial Hospital rose like a pile of bones, the remains of some animal that had fallen down behind the acres of trees that surrounded it and never gotten up.

On the other side of the rotunda, he saw workmen on scaffolding and ladders, hammering sheets of plywood across the windows, filling the evening air with the reassuring *tap-tap-tap* of endless American labor. They'd been working all week, covering every door and window to dissuade any thieves or vandals who would soon be tempted by Tanglewood's unwatched grounds, and now the work was virtually complete. The entire building was boarded shut in an irregular crossword puzzle of wooden planks.

In two hours it would be dark. It was the Fourth of July weekend, temperatures in the mid-nineties with the kind of humidity that gave even the lightest fabrics an itchy, clutching dampness. Mike continued along the walkway, the moist heat creating little sweat blotches on the front of his blue scrub pants, and stopped outside the main entrance, where two men in yellow hard hats were packing up the last of their tools and carrying them to a waiting pickup.

"Almost done?" Mike asked.

"Just about," one of the men said, not bothering to look up.

"How are people getting through?"

The hard hat nodded vaguely off to the right. "Emergency room exit."

Mike followed the cement path beneath the long overhang where for decades ambulances had dropped off casualties. Exchanging sun for shadow, his eyes lost their squint and his face softened, becoming younger, friendlier.

He was thirty-four years old, an age that had once seemed as insurmountable as Everest but now felt as lived-in as his old beach sandals. Parenthood had added the first wrinkles around his eyes, and his hairline was beginning to thin. Lately, without saying anything about it, Sarah had begun buying low-fat snacks and sending salads with his supper, which he knew was as close as she'd ever come to remarking on the fact that they were both, unthinkable as it once seemed, broaching the hinterlands of middle age.

Mike went inside, walking past Steve Calhoun in his alcove set just within the emergency room entrance.

"Seven o'clock already?" Calhoun asked, scowling down at the Sports page.

"Almost."

"Ain't you the eager beaver." The security guard shook his head. "My old man said never trust a fella that isn't late for work once in a while."

"Sounds like the model employee."

"Then there's you," Calhoun continued on, "never been a minute late in your life. Coming in early, even." He seemed to mull it over in his mind. "Man like that must have something real special waiting for him downstairs."

"Excuse me?"

"Come on, sweet Jolie Braun?"

Mike flushed. "Now listen—"

"Okay, take it easy," Calhoun said, looking up from his newspaper to nod at the wall of video monitors rising alongside him. "I get paid to notice things, that's all. Doesn't mean I got to tell nobody." A smile crept over his face. "You're a married man, ain'tcha? Got a kid at home?"

Mike set his hands on the security counter and leaned forward, forcing Calhoun to meet his eyes. "You're way off base on this."

"Not that I blame you. Lord knows I'd give my left one to get my hands around some of that."

"Look—"

"All right, all right, don't get all bent out of shape." Calhoun leaned back on his rickety stool and Mike heard the big key ring on his belt jingle. "You know, I'm surprised they even made your sorry ass come in to work tonight. You must have really pissed somebody off up the food chain, huh?"

Mike blew out his breath, relieved at the turn in conversation. "Must have."

"And the midnight shift no less?" Calhoun scowled at him, the incredulity building in his eyes like an impending sneeze. "Christ Jesus, there ain't even anybody here! Ambulance fleet transferred the last patients out to Good Sam's this morning. All that's left is files and furniture. Otherwise this whole place is as hollowed-out as my checking account."

"Suits me." He watched Calhoun's hand move automatically to the breast pocket of his uniform, finding the soft-pack of discount cigarettes, shaking one out and installing it expertly between his lips. Though he couldn't have been much older than Mike, Calhoun's entire physical appearance betrayed a lifetime of spectacular misuse and neglect. He was a scrawny, limping, unshaven man with an enormous Adam's apple who nonetheless evoked a kind of brute durability, as if the very ligature of his body was strung together by alcohol-cured leather.

For the three years Mike had worked at Tanglewood, Calhoun's "office" had been a gauntlet that he had to run just to get to the time clock. Here the security guard sat with his keys, cigarettes, and closed-circuit video feeds from every corner of the hospital, as protected as any endangered species: the gainfully employed American functional alcoholic. And from the current smell of things, Calhoun hadn't waited until he was home to start drinking.

*Let him say what he wants about Jolie Braun,* Mike decided. Nobody would believe him anyway.

"Ayuh." Calhoun grinned in a way that made his long chin appear to grow even longer. "I guess you ought to have it quiet tonight." He looked around with the comical bewilderment of the person the universe had chosen as its straight man more often than not. "But I still don't see why they couldn't give you one night off."

"I appreciate your concern." Mike was already leaning into the first step that would carry him away from Calhoun and whatever remained of this conversation when he heard rubber squealing up the service road in front of the hospital. Turning, he saw a line of police cruisers pulling into the rotunda, followed by an ambulance. Officers in blue uniforms were already getting out, moving with the swift urgency of men about their work.

Calhoun glanced up. "What the hell is all this happy crap?"

"Got your patient here," a young cop in sunglasses said, walking up, thrusting a fat stack of pages in Calhoun's direction.

"Hold it." Calhoun put down his paper and stood up. But the EMTs were already opening the back of the ambulance, unloading a stretcher with a man in an orange prison jumpsuit strapped to the rails. The man stared into the blue summer sky with an absolute vacancy of expression that seemed to Mike's eye neither childlike nor tranquil. Like the hospital, he thought, the man on the stretcher looked dead.

"Says here he's going for an MRI," the sunglasses cop said. "Either you two geniuses know where that is?"

Mike nodded. "I work there."

"Yeah? Well, that makes you my new best friend."

Craning his neck, Mike tried to get a better look at the face of the man strapped to the litter, but the shadows of the officers surrounding him continued to float over his features, obscuring them like a series of ill-fitting masks. It felt like the man's face was hiding from him, ducking away just when he thought he might catch a glimpse of it. The cops, all five of them, stood looking at one another across the stretcher. Mike realized that the paramedics had already climbed back into the ambulance; within moments the vehicle sped off, leaving them there with the silent passenger.

"Who is this guy?" Mike asked.

Nobody said a word.

The elevator doors jumped open and the cops came out with the stretcher—Calhoun had elected to stay upstairs—when Mike saw Jolie waiting for them. She was holding a digital camera, snapping photos of the man in the prison jumpsuit until the sunglasses cop gave her a hard look.

"If I were you I'd put that away," the cop said. "That flashing light's liable to make our friend here lose his happy thoughts." He was still wearing his tinted aviator specs, despite the fact that he was now underground. "You put our boy here in an agitated state, it's gonna get ugly in a hurry." Without waiting for Jolie to reply, he looked over at Mike. "Which way we headed, chief?"

"That way," Mike said in a voice that, to his own ears, sounded lost amid the unexpected flurry of activity. He hadn't learned anything about the man on the stretcher, or why Jolie would want to take his picture, but he had finally gotten a clear look at the prisoner's face in the elevator. It made him feel cold all over. Though the man still wore no expression, he could feel the green eyes watching him, drifting away and coming back again with the lazy watchfulness of a predator sizing up his prey.

They pushed the stretcher past the vacant X-ray and fluoroscopy suites, the waiting room, and a CAT scan whose door stood open to reveal the green glow of the control panel shining across the tile floor. The long hall ahead was empty except for a broken wheelchair and a stack of cardboard boxes. Mounted to the wall was a digital punch-clock, and Mike swiped his badge without breaking stride.

"Through those double doors." He pointed with his chin. "There's a button on the wall."

One of the cops hit the button and they wheeled the litter into a larger space whose dimly lit perimeters receded into darkness. Monitors and computer equipment lined the walls, and Mike heard the low hum of climate-control systems cycling fresh air through the ventilation ducts. Thirty feet in front of him, behind a square of tinted glass, was the scan room, the six-foot bore of the 1.5 Tesla Philips magnet gaped like an open mouth.

He dropped his backpack on the floor and kicked it aside, out of the path of the stretcher.

"What's this?" The sunglasses cop reached behind a desk and pulled up an aluminum baseball bat. "You and Florence Nightingale play ball down here when it gets slow?"

Jolie shook her head, pointing through the glass. The entire entourage paused to look at her. "There's twenty miles of copper wire coiled up inside that bore that holds a constant electrical charge," she smiled broadly, clearly happy to have everyone's attention. "And the guys that installed the emergency vent were more interested in my chest than getting the shaft put on straight. If the chamber ruptures and the backup vent fails, we've got three seconds before helium gas fills the room. That's where Mr. Louisville here comes in." She pantomimed someone swinging a bat toward the glass.

The cop leaned over toward Jolie, and Mike was just close enough to hear him speak into her ear. "I can sympathize with those guys who installed the vent." He took off his sunglasses. "You got a boyfriend?"

"I dated a cop once. It didn't work out."

"Yeah?"

"I wouldn't let him bring his gun to bed."

The cop said, "You serious?" and Jolie started saying something about handcuffs, as Mike glanced around the scan room, taking stock of the remaining equipment. Sitting out on the table next to the console was a foil-wrapped bottle and two plastic champagne flutes. It was just odd enough to jar him back into the flow of Jolie's one-woman show, the kind of "here I am, boys" performance piece she could carry on almost indefinitely, given a willing audience of men.

"Hey, Jo?" He nodded at the champagne. "What's that?"

A twinge of secrecy shadowed the corners of her lips. "Didn't you get my note?"

"I got it," Mike said and felt a prodding finger of unease whose source he couldn't quite pinpoint. "What's with the snapshots?" Out of the corner of his eye, he saw the other cops once again pushing the stretcher toward the MRI door.

"I'm going to sell them on eBay. Candid photos of serial killers go for a lot of money."

"Serial killers?" He looked at her more closely, wanting to see teasing in her face but not spotting any. "Who ordered this?"

"Dr. Walker." Jolie turned to where the cops had stopped with the stretcher and pointed at the door. "Guys, hold up."

A red sign there read:

> WARNING—THIS MAGNET IS ALWAYS ON!
> ABSOLUTELY NO LOOSE METAL OBJECTS!
> "DO WE HAVE YOUR KEYS?"

"All those metal restraints are going to have to come off Mr. Snow before we put him into the magnet," Jolie said. "You big strong men might as well get started stripping him down."

"Mommy, where are we going?"

"To the hospital to see Daddy." Sarah had answered this question three times already since they'd left the house twenty minutes ago, and it was part of a routine so familiar that it hardly registered. In any case, her mind was preoccupied with more pressing matters.

They were on Route 72, having finally cut away from the herd of holiday traffic coming off the turnpike, deep into soybean fields and grain silos that gave this landscape its texture. Some of the silos had Bible verses painted on the side, most had American flags. On the Outback's passenger seat, an empty cardboard box rode shotgun. Sarah told herself that she was dropping by to pick up whatever Mike had stored in his locker—books, clothes, coffee cups, the menagerie of personal items he'd accumulated after working three years at Tanglewood. But if she was going to be even remotely honest with herself, that wasn't the real reason for her visit tonight.

Faintly, she heard her mother's voice ringing through her head: *Once a cheater, always a cheater. Because they know they can.* The smug confidence of that voice always made her cringe. *Once a cheater, always a cheater. Because they know they can. Because they—*

"Stop it," she said, under her breath, but still loud enough that Eli picked it up from the backseat. He'd always had her sense of hearing.

"What, Mommy? What did you say?"

"Nothing."

"You said 'stop it.' "

"Just talking to myself." She turned off 72 onto Mill Valley Road, and up ahead in the distance, through the tree line, she could just barely make out the cracked concrete tablelands of Tanglewood's outermost parking lots gleaming in the sun. "We're almost there."

"How much longer?"

"Five minutes."

The cell phone in her canvas MasterCard bag started chiming Beethoven's "Ode to Joy," a custom ring-tone that she had personally programmed in but nonetheless always sounded slightly off-key. Digging past a box of Eli's animal crackers, she pulled out the cell, thumbing the "talk" button before she'd even checked the number.

"Hello?"

"Sarah?"

Her mother: Sarah felt herself struggling for normalcy. "What's up?"

"Where are you, dear?"

"Going to visit Mike."

"Everything all right?"

"Fine."

"Your voice sounds funny."

"It's this pollen count," Sarah said, already wishing she hadn't picked up the phone. "And the reception's about to go out. What's up?"

Newspaper rustled in the background, a TV crackled from the other room. "Your father wants to know what time you're coming over for lunch on Monday. He's doing steaks on the grill."

"I'm not sure we'll be there."

"We picked up sparklers for Eli and some of those lamb kebabs from the Greek place. How many do you think you'll eat?"

"I don't know if we'll make it," Sarah said. "I'll have to let you know."

"I'm sending your father to the store now. If—"

"Mom, please, all right? I'm about to lose reception."

Now there was no mistaking the weight of the silence hanging on the other end. Sarah could think of nothing to fill it that wouldn't make it worse.

"All right," her mother said finally. "Let us know."

"I will."

"Give Eli a kiss from Nana."

"Right."

"You're sure you're all right?"

"Mom—" Just as she felt the last strand of her patience slipping through its pulleys, it occurred to her that there might actually be something else, an unspoken reason why her mother had called. "Is something wrong?"

Her mother was quiet for a moment. "No," she said finally. "I just woke up with one of my feelings this morning. I wanted to make sure you and Eli and Mike were all okay."

Sarah sighed. Despite everything, her mother's concern sounded genuine. "Thanks for calling. I'll talk to you later, okay?"

"Bye, honey."

Sarah closed the phone and set it aside with a heightened sense of unease. Her mother's "feelings" came often enough that she rarely put stock in them, but once or twice—

"Mommy?"

She looked up. Mindless routine had taken her to the hospital's sprawling employee parking lot, empty except for a discarded McDonald's cup in the middle. Sarah realized that tonight she could park wherever she wanted. Nobody was going to ticket the Outback for taking up space in the ER lot on the last night the hospital was open.

"Yes?"

"Who was on the phone?"

She turned up the service drive, past the visitor lot, swung in alongside the main building. "Nana."

"What'd she say?"

"Just calling to say hi," she said, mindful that her son had listened to every word of her end of the conversation. She waited for further questioning on the subject, but instead Eli asked:

"Did we bring Daddy dinner?"

"No."

"Then why are we going to see him?"

She caught her son's face in the rearview mirror, put on a smile. "It's a surprise."

*You can say that again.*

They got out, Eli holding her hand all the way to the entrance. The hospital's flag was down but the cable clanged against the steel pole. Sarah didn't realize that Eli had been imitating the noise, softly, under his breath, until they got inside.

Mike found Walker by the vending machines next to the ground-floor elevator, struggling to feed a wrinkled dollar bill into a coffee machine. He watched him thumb the creamer button several times, apparently not realizing the machine had already spit his dollar back at him.

"I think it's empty."

The tall man in the white coat flinched, visibly startled, and removed the dollar from the slot with a sheepish smile that looked completely out of place on his face. He was in his mid-sixties, with the finely chiseled, almost aristocratic features that made Mike wonder, on more than one occasion, what the rest of the world must look like from up there. Army ants? Chess pieces? Or something even more impersonal, components that Walker constantly strove to align according to his vision?

"Mike." He smiled. "Didn't hear you coming."

"You brought in Frank Snow on our last night of operation?"

The doctor's eyes lit from deep within. "He's here?"

"Jo's putting him on the table right now."

"I'll have to examine him before he goes in." Walker began walking quickly up the hall toward the MRI suite. "Apparently Mr. Snow's been experiencing headaches and numbness."

Mike found himself hurrying to keep up. "We could've waited until the Harrisburg scanner was up and running. Hell of a thing to spring on us on our last night."

"Just a routine brain MRI," Walker said, opening the door into the suite. "Thirty minutes and he won't be our problem anymore."

"Somebody should have told the ambulance drivers that," Mike said, letting a hint of irritation creep into his voice. "They couldn't wait to get out of here."

Walker gazed at him placidly. In front of them, the man on the stretcher held up his arms so the police could remove his handcuffs.

"I've never apologized for making anyone do their job. I don't intend to start now." At length the doctor took a syringe from his pocket and began filling it from a bottle whose label Mike couldn't read. "Mr. Snow's other symptoms include generalized weakness, with multiple incidents of dizziness, lethargy—"

"My heart goes out to him." Mike looked over at Jolie as she turned to the detainee and took another photo. It looked like one of the cops was about to move to stop her, but the officer with the sunglasses held him back. *Guy must really think his chances are pretty good,* Mike thought. The flash danced over the prisoner's indifferent face, glinting off something deep and broken in his eyes, and a moment later Mike felt the emotional aftershock like a rumble of thunder after lightning.

Frank Snow: he knew the name. Anyone watching the news ten years ago would have recognized it—a synonym for when things went so wrong the adjectives no longer sufficed. Knowledge of the man's crimes felt both practical and primordial, a built-in cautiousness that came along with a grown-up fear of dark places and sudden noises. Mike didn't even have to actively engage his memory to recall grainy newspaper photos of a remote barn with black-stained ropes and chains on the floor, notes, piles of clothes, and sneakers in one corner.

Snow turned his head toward Jolie's camera, the flash leaping off his skin. A vein twitched in the back of his hand and Mike saw what looked like needle tracks on his arm, some possibly infected. Who knew what kind of diseases Snow might've picked up in prison? Had anybody even bothered obtaining an adequate medical history? He was suddenly struck by the realization that everything about this procedure felt poorly thought out by people with no stake in the outcome.

An older cop, who had introduced himself as McPhee, removed the last of the leg restraints. He glanced briefly at Jolie, narrowed his eyes, and turned toward Mike. "Ready when you are."

Mike put on a pair of rubber gloves and walked over to Snow, who stood gazing back at him, expressionless once more, though now it seemed to come from deep within a man who had abandoned his body completely. His eyes were warehouse-empty. Within arm's reach, Mike smelled a churchgoer's bouquet of aftershave and the eye-watering sting of eucalyptus mouthwash.

"This way," he said, nodding Snow through the doorway. Beyond it was the room where the scanner sat waiting, a long, narrow table protruding like a white tongue. Silver foil ventilation pipes squirmed from the top of the plastic housing straight up to the ceiling, where they passed between floors and eventually to the outside world.

The last ten steps to the scan table seemed to take forever. Snow shuffled forward as if shackled to the air itself. His head hung down, eyes to the floor, and as he turned to sit on the table, Mike noticed something rising from his collar up the back of his neck.

It was the spiny crest of a black serpent, its scales and pigmentation painstakingly engraved in a mesh of lines that must have taken months to accomplish. What would such a thing look like fully revealed? Had Snow gotten it done before he'd been caught? What Mike glimpsed now already looked far too sophisticated for prison ink.

"Lie down on your back," he said, keeping his voice as flat as possible. "The test takes approximately thirty minutes. You'll hear a series of loud knocking sounds, like a jackhammer. During that time you should hold perfectly still." He settled headphones over Snow's ears and slid the plastic head coil down over the man's face, where it fit like a mask. "If you move during the scan . . ."

He hesitated, losing his train of thought. Snow's smell had changed somehow. The aftershave and mouthwash were gone, overcome by a thick, feral stink pouring through the prison uniform. When he glanced down, Snow was grinning at him, his green eyes bright now, lips skinned back to the gum line. His arm shifted sideways along the jumpsuit.

"I forgot to take this out of my pocket." Snow held up something, a folded silver square. "Mind holding on to it for me?"

Without really intending to, Mike felt himself reaching out and taking the thing. It was warm from Snow's pocket, soft like a stick of gum. Holding it as far from his face as possible, he slipped it into his own pocket and flipped the toggle switch on the side of the machine, raising the table and aligning the laser light just above Snow's eyes. The table slid deep into the mouth of the magnet until only Snow's feet stuck out, encased in beige canvas prison shoes. From here Mike could see Snow's fingers laced together on his chest, as poised as a corpse at a viewing.

"Oh, and don't worry about your son," Snow's voice drifted out from inside the tube. "I've got special plans for him."

Mike looked in. "What?"

Silence now, so unresponsive that Mike could almost have imagined the whole thing.

*He's messing with you.*

*Yeah, but how did he know—*

*Lucky guess. Just start this thing and get it over with.*

Mike left the room, closed the door behind him, and sat down to scan.

"What was he doing in there?" Jolie said. "Asking you on a date?"

"He stinks." Even out here, Snow's smell was stuck in his nose just as the killer's words were lodged in his head. Mike selected the first sequence and waited while the radio frequency amplifier started its warm-up on the other side of the glass. He couldn't stop thinking about how Snow had grinned at him from inside the head coil, eyes so bright they might see in the dark, and the way his smell had soured, thickening as the man snapped to life.

*Don't worry about your son.*

He took the silver square from his pocket, turned it over in his still-gloved hand. It was a piece of tightly folded paper, slightly damp, wrapped in grimy aluminum foil. He peeled the wrapper away, unfolded the paper.

It was a torn-out page from a hard-core skin magazine, its once-glossy sheen so faded and creased that Mike couldn't tell the gender of the bodies depicted on it, only that they were all naked and complexly knotted together in twos and threes. There were words written sideways across the pictures.

Holding the page under the desk, Mike turned it lengthwise to read. Black marker was scrawled across the page forming thick crooked letters, a hasty child's handwriting:

*You have a choice. Stay and do your job or take your family and get out. Make this decision RIGHT NOW. You won't get another warning.*

Mike frowned, read the note again, not comprehending. His family wasn't even—

"Whoa, Mike, he's already moving," Jolie said. Mike looked up through the glass into the scan room. Deep inside the tube of the magnet, Snow's knee had started to bounce.

*You won't get another warning.*

Behind him, he heard a voice say, "Daddy!"

Mike spun in his chair and saw Eli running toward him, carrying his water bottle in one hand and a box of animal crackers in the other. Falling into his arms, the boy clasped him furiously in a tumble of smells and small muscles, love so intense it almost hurt. Mike looked up over his son's head where his wife stood holding an empty box.

"Mike." Her eyes flashed off Jolie, the bottle, two glasses. "We need to talk."

"Not now." Inside the magnet, Frank Snow had drawn his legs up so all that was visible was the lower half of his legs. Mike hit "Abort Scan" and the knocking sound stopped. "You have to get out of here."

She was rooting around in her purse. "Mike—"

"Sarah, you have to leave!"

Now she looked up, face smooth with shock. Eli had drawn back to stare at him, speechless. Even the cops, who were crammed at the door of the scan room, momentarily turned their heads around in surprise.

"Go upstairs; I'll meet you in the lobby. Find Steve Calhoun. He'll keep an eye on you until I get a chance to come up."

At first Sarah didn't move. Then with no visible change in expression she dumped her bag on the floor, pouring out a wallet, wads of Kleenex, toy trains, a cell phone, fruit snacks, parking tickets, slips and scraps of paper that skittered in front of her. Mike saw her Coach key chain hit the worn tile, the one he'd given her on their first anniversary. Reaching down, Sarah picked up a crumpled slip and tossed it at his feet.

"I found this in your pocket last night," she said. Her voice had a drab, resigned flatness that he'd heard only once before in their marriage.

"Sarah—". Too many things were happening at once. His wife had turned into an ice sculpture in front of him. Somewhere off to his right, Jolie was talking again, saying something to the police, but it no longer sounded remotely humorous, and the cops were all talking simultaneously.

"Sarah," Mike said, "wait!" But she was already shoving piles of stuff blindly back in her bag. She grabbed Eli's hand, pulling him away, the boy twisting around to look back at Mike. Mike dropped the note, shot to his feet sharply enough to send his chair rolling backward, where it banged into the desk. He looked over at the others. "I'll be right back."

Jolie stared; no one else seemed to notice. "Wait, you're leaving *now*?"

"Just get the scan started. See if you can make him hold still."

"I'm not even on the clock anymore. The only reason I even stayed—"

He was out the door before she finished, into the empty hallway. There were three different ways Sarah and Eli could've gone, but he knew she wouldn't have taken the elevator. Swinging open a metal door to the stairs, he looked up just in time to see a sliver of daylight disappearing through the door at the top.

"Sarah?"

She didn't stop.

"Sarah, wait."

From behind him, Jolie's voice, shrill with alarm: "Mike! You need to get back here, now!"

He spun around and saw the cops and Dr. Walker charging into the hall with Frank Snow on a stretcher. Even from this distance, Mike could see Snow's body convulsing so violently that the cops had to hold him down on either side. One of his prison shoes sailed off his foot and hit the wall.

"Get the elevator!" Walker yelled.

"What happened?" Mike hit the button. "Where are you going?"

"There's a ventilator up on six." Walker bent, tilted Snow's chin back, and put his mouth against the plastic protective ring he'd placed over the other man's lips, giving Snow a breath. Snow's chest went up and down. His arms dangled down limp, and Mike saw that the man's eyes were rolled so far back in his head that they showed only glossy whites. The smell rolling off his skin was more redolent than ever, throbbing up Mike's nasal passages until his eye sockets ached.

"Jolie's done for the night. We're going to need you to go with us," Walker said.

Mike hesitated, trying to put his thoughts in order. *What is going on around here?* In the midst of all this, he found his attention drawn back to the door where he'd last seen Sarah and Eli. But he knew they were already gone.

Steve Calhoun was again staring at the Sports page, trying to make the box scores line up, when Mike's wife and kid came hurrying out the emergency exit, her long legs scissoring, the boy's little legs scurrying to keep up.

"Leaving already?"

That didn't even slow her down. Calhoun had a nice buzz going from the Old Crow he'd been tippling into his coffee since around three, first a couple drops and then a little more until his mind felt light and buoyant, a long pop fly sailing upward in the summer night.

"Hey," he said louder. "Everything okay?"

This time she did stop, holding the boy's hand, and looked back over her shoulder. Eight o'clock light was reaching up the hallway, golden hues illuminating the individual strands of hair that had come loose from her ponytail, and Calhoun thought, *Why the hell would anybody want to cheat on that?*

"Excuse me?"

"You all right?"

Funny how things clicked together—how had he missed it before? Marching through here a few minutes earlier, she'd been all business. Three minutes later she and the kid were back. Nothing good ever ended that fast. Three minutes was all the time it had taken for Steve Calhoun's own parents' marriage to explode, spraying shrapnel that still hadn't been found. Three minutes and half his childhood, the half he could remember.

She was still looking at him. In his half-lit state, it didn't seem weird to be looking at Mike Hughes's pretty wife and thinking of his own mother throwing a bottle of whiskey at his old man as she grabbed little Stevie's arm and yanked him out the door so hard he'd felt his shoulder pop.

"Do you know my husband?" she asked.

"Mike?" He nodded. "Sure."

"What's going on with him and that woman Jolie? And what are all those cops doing downstairs?"

"Nothing." Calhoun had never felt more convincing in his life. "They're just coworkers. And the cops were escorting some poor cracked-out bastard who needs to have his head looked at. Ain't too friendly, are they?"

Sarah tilted her head up, what Calhoun first took to be scrutiny. Then he realized she was looking at the great bank of video screens that formed the wall behind him, a mosaic of black-and-white images, empty hallways, vacant waiting rooms, doors, stairwells—all of them still and ghost-ship deserted.

Sarah looked at his ID tag. "Mr. Calhoun, is it?"

"Steve."

"Are there cameras down in the MRI department?"

"Sure, you bet." He allowed himself a touch of irrational pride, as if having the whole place under surveillance was somehow his doing. "There's cameras everywhere."

"Show me."

"I'm really not supposed to—"

"Please." Sarah gave him a smile that was more of a wince, the expression of a woman covering up a deep bruise. "I need to see."

Calhoun looked down at the little boy who was clinging to her hand, gazing up at her, and realized with a lurch that he *was* that boy. Not that they'd changed bodies or anything Freaky Friday like that, but the odd, lost look in the kid's face matched the feeling of dismay sinking into his own heart. The booze evaporated so suddenly that he felt a lump rise in his throat where the right words should have been.

Without much hope, he put his fingers on the keyboard beneath the bank of monitors and typed in the surveillance code for the MRI suite. One of the monitors flicked over to show a deep, empty room with the scanner at the far end.

"Nobody there?" she asked.

"Guess not," Calhoun said, wondering if he sounded as relieved as he felt.

"But I was just down there. What happened to everybody?"

"Mommy," the little boy said restlessly, squinting at the screen. "Where's Daddy?"

"Hold on." With a grunt, Calhoun got up off his shaky stool and typed again, thick fingers bumbling off the keys. Onscreen, the camera angle flipped lengthwise, showing the suite from the opposite direction. From the right, a figure moved across the waiting room, the normalcy of it made strange by the declarative flatness of the raw video feed.

It was Jolie. Calhoun watched her walk up to a row of employee lockers, putting in a key and opening it up to get her things out. From time to time he and some of the guys watched her down there—the Jolie Broadcasting Channel was what they called it, as in, *Let's see what's playing on JBC*—but never with another woman looking over his shoulder.

"She's all by herself," Calhoun said, fully aware that Sarah's primary interest was Jolie, rather than the handful of boys in blue.

"Hold on," Sarah said, not looking away from the screen. "Is there a better angle?"

Calhoun shook his head. When it came to watching Jolie, he knew all the angles.

"Is Daddy on TV?" The boy had clambered halfway up Calhoun's stool, balancing on it for a better look.

"You want to be careful up there, partner," Calhoun said. "That thing ain't real steady." He looked over to see if Sarah was going to say anything, but she was still watching Jolie on the monitor.

"You're sure there's not a better view of the room?" she asked.

"Why? I told you—"

"There's someone else down there."

Calhoun scowled. "There is?"

"Look." Sarah pointed at the upper corner of the screen, where a blurry swarm of pixels hovered immediately behind Jolie's back, just a shadow outside the camera's scope. At first Calhoun didn't see it, but when he got closer, sure enough, there was the outline of a man in profile standing behind her at the edge of the digital void.

"That's not Mike, is it?" she asked.

"I don't think so."

"Is there some kind of intercom you could call down there with?"

"It's in the operator's office."

A vivid red light began to pulse on the control panel next to the keyboard.

"What's that?" Sarah asked.

"Dammit." Calhoun checked the label above the blinking light. "Something's wrong."

## 7

They hadn't overloaded the elevator; even with Walker and the cops onboard along with Snow, they still weren't anywhere near its four-thousand-pound weight capacity. Yet the cables had shuddered to a halt just the same, the car jolting like it had struck something halfway up the shaft, everybody jammed together so closely that Mike could feel the officers on either side of him sucking in a breath.

"Somebody forget to pay the electric bill?" one of them asked.

Nobody laughed. Mike looked at the control panel, where half the lights had come on at once in an irregular checkerboard that reminded him somehow of the boarded-up windows outside. The change in atmosphere was instantaneous. A moment earlier a big officer named Oz had been teasing Repko, the sunglasses cop, about leaving Jolie behind downstairs, while Repko treated all of them to a long and loving description of what he'd do to Jolie given a moment of privacy. Now the banter was done, and Mike sensed air molecules getting stickier, a mesh of stale atmosphere. On the litter in front of them, Snow twitched and rolled his eyes, made a low foggy groaning sound through barely parted lips. White curds of spit formed at the corners of his mouth and he opened and closed his jaws with a series of sticky smacking sounds. His smell had become almost palpable now, a moist second layer that pressed against Mike's skin. Walker leaned forward, gave Snow another breath through the plastic CPR shield, watched his chest go up and slowly fall again, then checked his pulse.

Mike reached past Officer Repko to the control panel and picked up the red telephone. It beeped twice and he heard Calhoun's voice on the other end: "Security."

"Steve, Mike. We're stuck in the east elevator."

"Say again?"

"We're in here with the patient and the thing just stopped. We're some-where between the fourth and fifth floors. He's not breathing. We're on our way up to get the vent."

"Hang on," Calhoun's voice said. "Let me check something."

"Hurry up."

"I'm the only one here, remember?" Calhoun sounded unmistakably agi-tated at being told what to do. "It's going to take me a minute. Let me check the main generator."

Walker gave Snow another breath, glanced up. "What's he doing?"

"Checking the power," Mike said, annoyed at Walker for getting him into this mess, but even more irritated at himself for agreeing to get onto the eleva-tor instead of going after Sarah. Even as he said it, the lights flickered and the whole car dropped—not far, only a foot or two, but abruptly enough that Mike heard himself gasp out loud as he dropped the phone and gripped the stretcher to hold on. When the lights came back on, the cops looked badly jarred, the way Mike thought they might appear if shaken from a deep and unpleasant dream. Even Dr. Walker's face reflected an element Mike had never seen before, the composed doctor actually caught off-guard, maybe for the first time ever.

On the stretcher, Snow's chest shook and rattled. Mike could feel the cops drawing away from the litter with nowhere to go, squeezing back against the walls. Someone said, "I should've been home by now." Someone else said, "Son of a bitch better not start puking." Of the group, only Walker stood his ground, administering breaths and keeping two fingers on Snow's throat to monitor his pulse.

Mike picked up the phone again. "Calhoun?"

There was a faint murmur, nothing he could make out. Sarah would've been able to hear it, but Mike's ears weren't that good.

*"Steve?"*

The line was dead. Slowly Mike placed the receiver back on its wall-mount with a hand that seemed to float like a balloon. Up until now he'd felt confu-sion, frustration, anger, regret, everything compacted into a kind of an-guished lump of disbelief that all of these things could go wrong on his last night of work. But this was different. It wasn't panic exactly, not yet, but . . .

On the stretcher, Snow's head rolled sideways and he spat out the plastic shield Walker had placed over his lips. The shield hit Repko's shirt and left a little spit stain in the shape of a perfect zero. From this angle it was impossible to say for sure, but Mike could have sworn he saw Snow grinning again.

The phone on the wall rang.

Jumping, Mike snatched it up, fumbling it back to his ear. "Steve?"

"Mike, listen," Calhoun's voice was faint and distracted, maybe a little slurry, "there's nothing wrong with the generator. It must be a problem somewhere in the elevator."

"How do we fix it?"

"Well, that's the trouble, I can't. I can make some phone calls, sure, but I don't know anything about—"

"Steve, listen to me, you have to get us out of here, all right?" Mike heard Dr. Walker giving orders to someone behind him. "Just tell me, is there any way out of this thing?"

There was a long pause, as if Calhoun were awaiting translation. Then: "It's an elevator, Mike. If you're stuck between floors, there's nothing I can do, you know, except like I said—"

On the stretcher, Snow's mouth was open, his throat producing a raspy crow noise. *Rraww.* It could have been an effort to breathe or—

*It could be laughter. He's actually laughing. He's laughing at us, trapped in here with him.*

"Rraww!" Snow cried. "Rraww!"

"What the fuck is this?" Repko asked.

Mike looked up. Even Walker had moved away from Snow now, staring at him from what little distance he could manage.

"Hey, Mike?" Calhoun's voice asked from far away. "You still alive in there, buddy?"

The elevator shook again, followed by the low underwater creaking sound of heavy weights straining against reluctant pulleys, and then, so slowly that it might have been an illusion at first, the car began to rise. Mike heard several sighs of relief from the cops.

"Steve? It's working again."

"Praise Jesus," Oz said, not sounding wholly sarcastic about it.

Through the receiver, Calhoun made a grunting sound. Somehow he sounded more disturbed now than he had a moment earlier. "I didn't do anything."

"Tell him to meet us up on six." Dr. Walker's voice was brusque. "I need him to unlock the equipment room up there for the vent." He paused as if considering whether to state the obvious: "And Mike?"

"Yeah?"

"Tell him to take the stairs."

**8.**

"You want some of this?" Jolie asked, holding up the bottle. "It's already lost its fizz."

She hadn't actually asked the older officer, McPhee, to stay down here with her in MRI while she packed her things, but she was grateful for his company just the same. All the other cops had gone up in the elevator with Snow and Walker and Mike Hughes, but their departure had left a void that made her jumpy, and she was not someone who was easily spooked.

McPhee shook his head. "I don't drink."

"It's just sparkling grape juice."

"Nah." From the sound, he was still on the other side of the suite, watching her. "Say, that's some tan you've got there."

"Thanks. My boyfriend says I'm going to get skin cancer if I'm not careful."

McPhee ignored the boyfriend reference, maybe didn't even hear it. "You go to one of those salons?"

"Sometimes."

"No tan lines, huh?"

Jolie gave him a dollar-store smile, the kind that any lonely guy worth his *Maxim* subscription would've read as a great big No Entry sign. "I don't believe in half-measures." Now she was just blathering, filling empty space while she packed the last few items from her locker: a spare scrub top, mouthwash, contact solution, a financial self-help paperback called *Prince Charming Isn't Coming*. "I'm ready if you are."

"Sure thing." McPhee pointed at the desk. "Hey, don't forget your camera. Looks expensive."

"Thanks." She gave him an actual smile and saw kindness amid the wrinkles of his face. Maybe she'd misjudged him, a lonely guy with no wedding band hoping for a few moments of stolen felicity with a woman half his age. "It can't be easy dealing with prisoners all day."

"I'm on the job," he shrugged. "Transporting this lowlife scumbag is just a favor to the DOC. Still"—he frowned, weighing the difference—"it ain't the Bahamas, that's for sure."

"I bet." Jolie cast one final glance around the MRI suite, bidding good-bye to a place she wasn't going to miss all that much. She glanced at the pile of papers Mike's wife had dumped from her purse, briefly considered picking them up. She wasn't doing Sarah Hughes any favors.

"I have to admit I almost stopped you from taking those snapshots of that son of a bitch," McPhee said. "They worth anything?"

"You bet."

"How much?"

"Let's just say he enjoys a certain cult following."

"Is that so?" McPhee hesitated, then seemed to arrive at a decision. "I got something here." He reached into his hip pocket. "Took it off of him as we were strip-searching him for his ambulance ride. You think something like this would be worth anything?"

Jolie looked at the piece of onionskin paper in McPhee's hand. It was a hand-drawn diagram, done in thin marker on the back of what she realized was a page torn out of a Bible. Cutting crosswise across the tiny lines of Scripture she saw lines and squares, numbers, arrows, and scrawled words in big spidery capital letters.

"Snow drew this?"

"Yeah, I guess." McPhee frowned. "Why, you know what it is?"

"Sure." Jolie nodded. "It's a map. Of the hospital."

**9.**

Sarah's eyes were still locked on the video monitors in Calhoun's security booth when Eli started screaming.

Just moments before, Calhoun had rushed upstairs to meet Mike and the others on the sixth floor, leaving them to watch her husband stuck in the now-moving elevator. "*There's Daddy!*" Eli had squealed, pointing at the monitor with heartbreaking excitement, "*Mommy, Daddy's on TV!*" And sure enough, there he was, packed in with the cops and a man in a prison uniform whose face disturbed Sarah in a way she couldn't have articulated intelligently, even under the most mundane of circumstances.

That's when the crash came, followed by Eli's scream, the shrillness of it bringing up the hairs on the backs of her arms. Pivoting, she saw him sprawled on the floor beside Calhoun's fallen stool. She could tell from his howling cry that he had really hurt himself, but she didn't know how bad it was until the bulge on his forehead started swelling just above his right eye.

"Oh, sweetheart." She knelt down next to him and tried to pick him up, but that only made him scream even harder, thrashing and pulling away as the pain got worse. "What happened? Let me see."

Normally, she would have identified that rickety stool as a potential hazard right away and kept Eli from climbing on it—even Calhoun had warned him about the thing—but today was no normal day. Today her mommy radar was adrift somewhere in the Bermuda Triangle, compass needles spinning, coordinates unknown.

"Shh, baby, it's all right," she said, not even able to hear herself anymore. He calmed a little, allowing himself to be held though he was still crying vigorously and wailing "Owwie, owwie," only wanting the hurt to go away. Sarah cradled him, rocking him gently, the way she had when he was little and colic kept him up through the night. After a few hitching breaths, he plugged his thumb into his mouth, a long-broken habit from infancy, and silenced himself.

"That's my big boy." Without realizing, she'd been crooning to him some made-up lullaby with nonsense words, train, spoon, gingerbread moon. At home he'd sit for an hour or more and listen while she played the piano, improvising a melody to keep him entertained. He gazed up at her now, face flushed and shining with sweat and tears, noisily squelching his thumb. "We'll get you fixed up, honey, okay? I promise we will."

But, oh the irony, here they were already in a hospital. Sarah brought him to her shoulder, stood up—there must still be icepacks, maybe even aspirin somewhere in the ER—and glanced at the video screens. The monitor she had been watching showed that the elevator was now empty, and she had hopes of seeing Calhoun or Dr. Walker somewhere down these ghostly gray halls.

*Or Mike.*

Yes, or Mike. And just how much of an all-day sucker did that make her? He'd promised her he'd come looking for them. Exactly how long did she plan on waiting down here for him? At this point it was safe to assume that he'd almost certainly forgotten they were here.

Except—

Except some infinitesimal hope-speck wanted desperately to believe otherwise. The hope was tiny but potentially catastrophic, a cancer cell, a third-world nation with a nuke. It was the same part that wanted what she'd found in Mike's pocket last night to be a colossal misunderstanding, the part that had wanted to believe him five years ago when he'd said, *No, of course not, I'd never do something like that, Sarah—Jesus, how could you even think such a thing?*

Five years ago and never quite the same after, despite his promise of never again. Five years of feeling like the security guard in a store full of incredibly fragile and expensive items, watching him so carefully, even after the baby came, knowing it was smothering him but somehow unable to stop.

*I'll meet you in the lobby.*

Had he actually said that?

Yes.

Did she believe him?

No.

So it was crazy, wasn't it, waiting here. She'd waited long enough. Eli was hurt, if she couldn't find a doctor on one of the TV screens she would drive Eli home, or to the outpatient center a mile from their house.

But what she saw instead made her stop and scowl in bewilderment.

Before her eyes, the surveillance monitors in Calhoun's booth began blinking out, one by one. Within seconds, every single one of them had gone dark.

Sarah picked up the phone next to Calhoun's keyboard, listened for the dial tone. It was dead.

"Mommy?" Eli croaked. "Can we go home? I want to go home."

She nodded. "We're leaving right now."

## 10

"Which way?" Calhoun asked. He was badly winded from the stairs, the blast furnace that was his chest wheezing so hard that if Calhoun hadn't been looking straight at them, Mike never would have guessed what he'd said.

"Follow me." Dr. Walker pushed the stretcher out of the elevator and into the empty hallway, past the nurses' station.

Six East was Pediatric Intensive Care. Children's drawings hung from the walls, fluttering as they passed, shaky crayon renderings of sunshine, dogs and cats, smiling kids in wheelchairs. They always made Mike wonder how many of the kids were already dead, leaving behind parents who took teddy bears to the graveyard.

Rounding the corner where the security guard had pointed them, he could already see that the hallway stretched out in front of them was also barren.

"Where's the vent?" he asked.

"Come with me." Walker yanked the front of Snow's stretcher forward, doubling their speed as they rattled down the hallway, the cops and Calhoun having to run to keep up with him. Mike frowned. Walker knew Peds ICU, and he must have known the hallway was a dead end—*Where was he going?*

At the end of the corridor, twenty feet beyond the last room, Walker skidded to a halt, spun the stretcher crosswise, and pointed at the wall.

Walker, to Calhoun: "Open this."

And Calhoun, squinting down at it, hands trembling as he struggled to catch his breath, fumbling for his enormous key ring: "Gimme a second."

Repko rolled his eyes, and Mike found himself wondering exactly how much the security guard had had to drink throughout the afternoon. At last he held up a key and wedged it into a nondescript hole, and a moment later Mike saw a door swing open to the right.

The space that was revealed was narrower than the doors that led to the patient rooms, Walker and Calhoun going in front and behind Snow's stretcher to fit through it. One of the cops followed and the door slammed shut behind them, seemingly of its own volition. But that didn't make sense, did it? Doors didn't do that.

Mike and the three remaining cops stood outside, looking at the closed door. There was an awkward high school dance moment where nobody seemed sure what to do. Repko cleared his throat, then Oz reached out, searching for some kind of latch or handle but finding only the keyhole, and hammered the area above the keyhole with his fist. "Open up." His head swiveled toward Mike. "What's going on in there?"

"I guess they're trying to get an airway."

"You work in this place, or what?" The cop pounded again. "Jimmy, it's Oz, open the door! Open the goddamn door!"

At first nobody said anything from the other side. Then, faintly, Mike thought he could hear a voice droning. He struggled to listen, but couldn't even tell who it was, let alone what was being said. Again he wished Sarah were here; she probably could've figured it out with ease. One of her favorite tricks when they had first started dating was identifying accidental notes in nature, the A-flat of a truck brake, the G-sharp of a fork hitting the floor. Any playful times were long gone, but Mike hadn't realized until now how much he still relied on her hearing. Life without it was sometimes like a foreign movie without subtitles.

Repko and the other officer were glancing around anxiously, but Oz had apparently already made his decision.

"Fuck it," he said. "Let's break the mother down."

Before the others could respond, the power on the sixth floor flickered, and in the space of a heartbeat, the walled-off, windowless passage fell into total darkness. Mike sucked in a quick breath of surprise and the lights came back on. Later, looking back on that first moment of blindness—surely no longer than a second or two—he thought he remembered an odd coppery flavor fluttering over the back of his tongue, no longer even panic but true fright.

*Talk about worst-case scenarios,* he thought, *a blackout at a time like this . . .*

But there was no need to worry. The power was back. He shoved the thought out of his mind and stood clear, watching as the cops prepared to knock down the door.

**II.**

By the time Sarah heard Jolie coming up the hall behind her toward the ER entrance, it was too late to pretend she hadn't noticed her. Jolie was carrying a grocery bag, walking alongside one of the cops, an older one with a gray mustache.

"What happened to the kid?" Jolie asked.

"He hit his head."

"He all right?"

Sarah adjusted her grip on Eli, not wanting Jolie to see his face. She looked like the kind of woman who would have something to say about a three-year-old sucking his thumb, and right now Sarah wasn't in the market for outside opinions on parenting, even from a doubtless expert like Jolie. She turned and headed for the exit.

"Where are you going?"

"Home."

"Hang on a second."

Sarah slowed her pace but didn't look back.

"I'm pretty sure there're icepacks in one of the storage closets on the other side of the ER," Jolie said. "I could go get one if you'd like. I think Officer McPhee here would be happy to wait with you."

The cop—McPhee—shrugged. "Sure thing."

Sarah stopped, feet frozen at the door while she reevaluated the lump on Eli's head, an ugly purple eye of accusation. Ice would probably make a difference on the long ride home.

"Well, you want me to get one?"

"Thank you," Sarah said. "I appreciate it."

"It won't take me long," Jolie chirped, as she set down the grocery bag. "You're such a good mommy. I can see what Mike saw in you."

Sarah felt the unmistakable feeling of lightness come into her cheeks that meant she was blushing. That was what did it, Jolie's casual flip-off as she twirled off to find medical supplies for Eli. It couldn't really be called a dig; the blade was much too sharp for that, an expertly administered jab so quick and sly the victim didn't feel it until she'd already started to bleed. Sarah turned back toward the exit again.

"Hey, hold up," McPhee's voice said behind her. "You aren't waiting?"

Sarah didn't reply, just carried Eli out into the warm twilight to the car. Birds twitted. In front of her, she could hear the *whang-whang-whang* of the flagpole cable, steadier now. A breeze was rising up.

"Mommy? What about Daddy?"

"He'll be home later." *Or not.*

Eli's eyes began to tear up afresh, Sarah thinking, *I can't handle this, not now, okay, please?* Setting him down outside the car, she cast one final look at the hospital. The last of the sun poured out long misshapen pools of darkness along the building's service drive. Overhead, a crow came down to meet its shadow on the roof.

"Shit."

Eli glanced up. "Shit?"

"My keys." Sarah pawed through her purse and emptied it out onto the hood. She had her wallet, a bundle of coupons and old receipts, and plenty of toy trains, but her keys weren't there. And the reason they weren't there, of course, was because she'd left them down in MRI, after Mike had rushed her out the door.

"Mommy?" Now the boy's bewilderment had seemingly eclipsed both his head pain and his sadness over leaving his father. "Where are we going now?"

"Back inside the hospital."

"Why?"

"Mommy forgot her keys in MRI."

"Why?"

"I just did, honey. Sometimes even grown-ups forget."

"Is Daddy down there?"

She sighed. "I don't know where your father is."

"Maybe we'll see him."

Clasping Eli in her arms, Sarah hurried from the car back inside the emergency room entrance. She'd expected someone to be there, but the hallway was now deserted.

# 12.

The kick that Oz gave the door didn't even budge it. *Weren't cops supposed to be good at kicking down doors?* Mike watched him stumble backward, catching himself on the opposite wall, off-kilter, angry, and probably a little embarrassed. "Son of a bitch," he muttered, hand going for his gun.

"Hey, whoa, Oz," Repko said. "Take it easy. Let's rethink this."

A loud crash came from inside the room, stopping them all where they stood like children in a game of statues. Mike heard somebody screaming, ending in a distant strangled gurgle. He felt a slow, luxurious wave of coldness move through him in a way he'd never experienced before—coldness that seemed to emanate from the inside out. *This is how a dying man must feel,* he thought. *That inner chill.*

The next sound that came from behind the door wasn't so much a sound as a shocking Fourth of July *boom* so low and deep that it pushed his eardrums in. Mike supposed he must have heard it—how could anything so huge and disruptive not make a sound? But the only auditory aspect he was aware of was the great gulf of silence that was left in its wake.

Oz looked up, his voice cracking in fright and bewilderment. "What the fuck was that?" Under other circumstances it might have been funny, such a tiny voice coming out of such a big man, but not now.

The door banged open, smoke flooding out, so thick and black that Mike didn't see Calhoun until Calhoun came spilling out at him with enough force to knock both of them backward in a tangle of limbs. In the instant he had to process everything, Mike saw that the man's face had blood on it, making his eyes even more wild and white. Calhoun looked like he wanted to scream but couldn't find the presence of mind to draw enough breath.

"Steve—"

Smoke was gushing out of the room now in great palpable billows, like squid ink. Mike's eyes and throat felt as if someone had rubbed hot lemons into them. Dropping to his knees, smearing away tears with the backs of his hands, he could just make out the legs of the cops as they forced their way into the room. He heard shouting and sooty coughing, and there was another scream that ended with terrible abruptness.

"Don't go in there!" Calhoun was now shrieking, somewhere off to Mike's right. He'd disappeared in the smoke, his voice growing smaller by the moment. "Don't go in!"

Whether they heard him, or simply couldn't go any farther, Mike saw the cops were now backing out as quickly as they'd gone in. One of them was vomiting down the front of his uniform; another stepped crushingly on Mike's hand as he went sprinting back down the hall.

*You have to get out of here. Right now.*

"Yeah," he said hoarsely. "Good idea."

Wrenching his head away from the doorway, he looked down the far end of the hall where they'd come from. It seemed very far away. He sucked in a deep breath, rose to his feet, and then he, too, began to run.

# 13.

Sarah was carrying Eli down the hall, her purse swinging on her elbow, banging into her hip, when she saw McPhee in the doorway up ahead. He looked at her in genuine surprise.

"Now what?"

"My keys," she said, not breaking stride. They were already far enough from the entrance and the emergency room that Jolie wouldn't see them unless she came looking in this direction. Sarah definitely didn't want to be around when the other woman came back. "I left them down in MRI."

He looked at her purse. "You sure about that?"

"Trust me, I—"

Something exploded, a tinkling thunderclap from above that shook the ceiling and stopped Sarah in her tracks. Her mouth said "What was that?" but she couldn't hear her own voice for a moment afterward, her ears ringing with whatever it was.

When her hearing came back, there was static blurting from McPhee's walkie-talkie, a panicked voice scratching from its speaker.

". . . into the room . . . some kind of explosion, he . . ."

McPhee unclipped the walkie-talkie from his belt, twisting the squelch button, trying to make the message clearer. Still the voices came in fits and starts, transmissions from another planet.

". . . God," another voice muttered, "what's—"

More static, heavier. Then:

"He's out! *He got out!*"

Sarah squatted down, setting Eli on his feet but holding his hand.

Through the radio she could hear a different voice, horribly frightened, screaming, "Don't go in there! *Don't go in there!*"

"Dammit," McPhee muttered, shaking the walkie-talkie now as if he could somehow jar its circuitry back in order. But the only thing coming out of the speaker now was irregular wafts of white noise.

"What's going on?"

"Mommy?" Eli asked. "What happened? Did something happen to Daddy?"

Sarah kept looking at McPhee, deflecting the question to him, but the cop wasn't playing. He was still holding the walkie-talkie up, but his right hand had fallen to his holster, unsnapping the strap across the pistol at his hip. He seemed to be processing many thoughts at once and verbalizing none of them.

"Officer?" Sarah stared at the cop's hand resting on his open holster. "What do they mean, 'he got out'? *Who* got out?"

McPhee's lips were moving silently, as if rehearsing lines. When he'd put them in the order that he wanted them, he met her stare. "I want you to leave."

"Where?"

"Back out to your car."

"I don't have my keys," she said. "That's why I—"

"Just go out to your car and wait there. Lock the doors. Stay there till backup arrives."

"You don't get it." Sarah shook her head. "My car's already locked, I always lock it. It's a habit. I can't get into it without my keys." She was clenching Eli's hand so tightly that he'd begun trying to pull away from her, and she made herself loosen her grip. "Now can you please tell me what's going on?"

"Mommy, what's—"

"We'll take care of it," McPhee cut in, pointing back at the ER entrance. "You just need to get out of here."

"Not until you—"

"We brought a prisoner in. If he's escaped, I can't let you stay here."

"Escaped?" It came out parched. "If he's already escaped, how do you know he's not outside the hospital? I'm not taking my son out there alone."

"Escaped?" Eli asked. "What's escaped?"

Sarah hadn't looked away from McPhee. "Who was he?"

"That's not important."

"Who was the prisoner?"

"Snow. Frank Snow."

"Snow?" Eli frowned. "In summertime?"

Sarah went weightless, felt a trapdoor swing open underneath her, click, and for a moment the only thing she was aware of was the stupid glugging thump of her heart in her chest, a gallon jug pouring out its contents.

"You're kidding."

McPhee gave her a bleak look.

"Frank Snow." The name moved slick and lethal through her insides, its innate wrongness triggering all sorts of chemical reactions, as if she'd inadvertently swallowed some kind of fast-acting poison. "That man is loose in this hospital and you want me to take my son out there alone?"

"We don't even know if—" For a split-second McPhee actually looked ready to continue the argument. Then his shoulders sagged a little. "Come along with me, then," he said. "We'll go down and get your car keys back."

Sarah lifted Eli back into her arms. He weighed close to forty pounds, but right now she raised him up with an ease she hadn't felt since carrying him home from the hospital just after he was born. His weight actually felt good, a confirmation of his substantiality and her own strength.

"Where's Snow, Mommy?"

She shushed him.

"Where's Daddy?"

"I don't know." She followed McPhee down the hall. An abnormal stillness seemed to surround them, the quivering, prefatory silence of fragile objects teetering on narrow shelves, a feeling remembered from childhood.

They turned right, away from the chapel, toward the cafeteria. Down the wide hallway, she could see the main lobby coming up, the part of the hospital that, with its big mahogany information desk, made her feel like she was entering some kind of grand hotel instead of a place where sick people went to either get better or die. Beyond it was the stairs they'd taken up from the ground floor.

"Stay close to me," McPhee said, not looking back over his shoulder.

"Why? Do you think there's—"

"Shh." Having clipped the radio back onto his belt, he was walking with his right hand on the butt of his pistol, though he hadn't drawn it from his holster.

Sarah realized her palms had started to sweat, her body already understanding what her mind had procrastinated over for too long. She looked at Eli. His expression of uncertainty and worry was now becoming flat-out terror. The lump on the side of his head made him look even more vulnerable, a child requiring comfort and reassurance that she had never felt less equipped to offer.

As they passed the information desk with its two empty swivel chairs facing the cavernous lobby, she looked ahead and saw that the door to the stairwell was slightly ajar, enough that she could see its rectangular wire-mesh window. McPhee must have seen it, too, because he stopped walking so suddenly that she almost ran into him.

"Mommy?" Eli whispered.

McPhee held up one hand and took another step toward the half-open door. Sarah saw that the gun, some kind of flat, standard-issue semiautomatic, had left his holster; now he was holding it upright with both hands at chest level. Seeing it exposed like that, its barrel glinting faintly under the lobby's track lighting, elicited a sense of gut-level immediacy in her that nothing else up until now had generated. She wondered if this was how civilians in war zones felt. *Nothing punctuates a moment like a weapon.*

"Police," McPhee announced, taking another step toward the half-open door. He'd begun a lateral move, crab-walking in a generous semicircle around the perimeter of the doorway, with his gun pointed out in front of him. "Who's there?"

Sarah felt Eli's arms tightening around her neck, making her aware of her own pulsing carotid. Hoisting him up higher to take the pressure off, she found herself moving backward in the direction of the information desk.

McPhee had stopped walking. His semicircular path had brought him directly in front of the half-open door, and after a moment of looking at whatever was behind it, he lowered the pistol and glanced back at Sarah. "It's stuck open."

"What?"

"Something's shoved under it on the inside. Hold on." Still moving carefully, he approached the door, bending down, and vanished behind it.

"Officer?" Sarah said.

McPhee reappeared holding a brown wedge of rubber. He was bracing the door open with his foot, and giving her an odd, relieved look. "Doorstop."

"It wasn't there when we came up."

"Maybe your husband stuck it there. Or that security guard, what's his name . . . Calhoun?" McPhee glanced behind the door again, down the stairwell. "There's another one down at the bottom of the landing. Hold on." He frowned, stepping behind the doorway again. "Wait, that's not . . ."

The door slid shut.

## 14

The ER supply cabinet was locked. After spending a few desultory minutes ransacking the nurses' station for the key, mumbling synonyms for "shit," Jolie had found herself faced with two equally unattractive alternatives. Either go back to Sarah empty-handed and admit defeat or go upstairs and try to find the kid an icepack on one of the floors.

*Or go home and take a bath.*

A tempting thought, one she would have pursued had it not been for the map that McPhee had shown her. Jolie couldn't stop thinking about the map. She'd made the mistake of telling McPhee it might be valuable, but she thought there might still be a chance he'd fork it over, if she showed him the right kind of good time. Snapshots of Frank Snow were one thing—she could eBay them for twenty bucks a pop, easy—but a hand-drawn map in Snow's own hand, written on a page out of a prison Bible? Who knew how much some nut would be willing to pay for that?

After all, Snow had been famous for his notes—his laborious handwriting scrawled on pages of either the Bible or porno magazines. Jolie even remembered seeing the notes reproduced on the news after his capture, with the more offensive language blacked out. The messages usually offered the victim some chance of survival, go or stay, run or hide, resist or cooperate. Devil's bargains. Almost none of his victims had managed to survive, but the few who had . . .

Those few told a different story.

Experts on every level had dismissed their testimonies as irreparably tainted by the trauma they'd undergone, but the handful who had somehow escaped had agreed to speak only under terms of strictest anonymity. Variously and inconsistently, they were said to have whispered of a thing whose abilities were weirdly restricted, an entity in human skin, unable to take what he wanted from his prey unless at some point they themselves chose to let it happen. Jolie had read the reports with incredulous fascination. It was pseudo-superstitious bullshit, no question, but it made the notes Snow wrote infinitely more valuable than the garden-variety psychobabble.

She went back up to the ER entrance, humming a Spanish flamenco song as she rounded the corner toward the exit.

"Okay, I've got some not-so-good news . . ."

Her voice trailed off.

They were gone.

McPhee, Sarah, the kid—all vanished.

The only thing Jolie found was the plastic grocery bag with her own things in it, the paperback, the mouthwash, her little digital camera, lying on the floor twenty feet from the front door.

She picked it up, irrationally hoping against hope that McPhee had stuck the map in there. Of course he hadn't. If she wanted it, she was going to have to find him and work for it. The question then became, how much did she really want the—

The explosion rang out distant but pervasive, a sonorous, rolling cloud of noise from the upper floors that made a sifting sound overhead, like hundreds of bricks subtly rearranging themselves. Jolie looked up as if there were something to see up there, but even the light fixtures looked normal.

She stood there motionless except for her eyes, feeling like the Felix the Cat clock she used to have as a kid, the one with the mischievous eyes and tail that swished back and forth, back and forth. First the missing map, now the big bang. In the life of Jolie Braun, in the ongoing litigation between curiosity and apprehension, curiosity always carried the day—it explained how she was always in so much trouble—and today was no exception. Map or no map, some part of her mind was already turning this into an anecdote to tell her friends at the bar: "I was working the last night before the hospital closed, when all of a sudden I heard this huge explosion . . ."

She headed upstairs to find out how her story was going to end.

Cradling Eli with both arms, Sarah started toward the door leading down the stairs where McPhee had just gone. The silence humming behind that door was bursting, scarcely containing the pressure.

"Officer McPhee?"

Less than ten feet away, she had already shifted Eli's body so she could reach for the door's handle with her right hand, when something struck it from the other side.

Whatever it was crashed into the door with one blunt thump, forcefully enough to knock it open a few inches and release a tiny gasp of cool air against her forearm. Sarah jumped back, dropped her purse, almost dropped her child, and screamed.

In her arms, Eli jerked with shock, and then he, too, screamed and burst into tears. He was clutching onto her with his arms and legs now, and Sarah turned and ran back toward the desk, hearing the thumping sound of something pushing the door open behind her.

There was another crash, and Sarah knew from the sound of it that the door was swinging open behind her. Whatever was on the other side, some animal, some thing, would be out now, and after them.

She moved without the luxury of thought. The information desk was right in front of her. Lunging forward, gripping Eli with both arms, she turned her body so that her shoulder knocked the swivel chair aside. She landed on one hip and rolled so that her son was on top of her. He was still bawling loudly, pulling on her shoulders and hair with great vehemence. She placed her hand firmly over his mouth and clamped it tight, looking straight into his eyes.

*We have to be quiet,* she thought, drawing him farther underneath the desk, as deep as they could go. She wanted to say this out loud to him, but whatever command of language she might've had earlier was gone. The thought wasn't truly a sentence but an abstraction, no more sophisticated than what must go through any animal's brain as it cowered from the hunter's scent.

*Who is it?*

*Snow? In summertime?*

Curled against her body, Eli gaped back at her. He was still crying, tears streaming down his cheeks, over her fingers, but whatever atavistic impulse he saw in her eyes had stopped him from sobbing.

*Must be quiet. Mustn't make a sound.*

With another thump, she heard the door open. Hydraulics hissed. For a moment there was silence. Then, gradually, came the muted jangle of loose metallic objects, moving closer.

B-flat. D-sharp. Then a note that wasn't a note at all, a ringing, muffled clink.

She already knew what they were.

Keys.

Above Sarah's clamped fingers, Eli's eyes widened, pupils twitching back and forth. His small body trembled against hers, strung tight with tension, both of them huddled deep beneath the information desk.

The jingling music of the keys approached, a random progression of sharps and flats. With every clink and rattle she could see them more clearly in her mind, a big metal ring with different shapes and sizes dangling off, twenty or thirty at least.

*Who carried so many keys? Calhoun.* But somehow she knew the hand that held them was not Calhoun's.

When they seemed like they couldn't get any closer, they stopped, as if the hand had suddenly clamped tight in a fist.

*Please, God, don't let him find us here.*

As if to imbed the thought permanently into this moment, she gazed into her son's face, imploring him again to remain quiet and still. She could smell something bad, something both sour and burned, clotting the air around her.

There was a correlative for it, but her jammed-up mind either couldn't or wouldn't provide it.

After an eternity, the jingling started again, the keys singing their cheerful little song off to her right, back toward the ER. Sarah listened as the sound dwindled, fading.

She lifted her hand from Eli's mouth. Her fingers had imprinted red bands across the lower half of his face. It was a face she'd gotten so used to seeing with a smile or a slight squint of curiosity, but now was only confused, pale, and scared, shining with tears. The purple knot above his eye was large and sad.

"Mommy," he whispered, "I don't want to do this anymore."

"Me either, baby."

"I want Daddy."

Sarah pushed herself out from under the information desk and moved into a squatting position. Eli was clinging to her furiously, chin digging into her shoulder. Peering up over the top of the desk, she saw that the lobby around them was empty and absolutely silent. If the jingling of the keys had been any indication, the person with them had gone the opposite way, into the ER, looking for a way out.

She looked across the lobby to the hall, the stairway door, at her purse on its side where she'd dropped it.

Their only way out was her own keys, the ones she'd left downstairs in MRI, and the only route there that she'd ever taken was the stairwell whose door she had just recently witnessed thudding with multiple unnatural impacts.

Still, they had to go.

Eli was shivering against her, little bird muscles trembling violently enough that they made his faint, tearful voice sound like he was stuttering. Her blouse was wet with his tears. "Muh-mommy? Whuh-what are we guh-gonna do?"

"We need to get the car keys," she said, holding him fast as she rose up to her full height.

"Now?"

She nodded. Abolishing all the reluctance she could from her mind, she started for the doorway. "Just cover your eyes, sweetie. Whatever you do, you just keep your eyes covered. You promise?"

"Yeah."

"Say, 'I promise.' "

"I puh-promise."

"All right." She got to the door, picked up her purse, and hooked it over her shoulder. She pulled the handle. "Here we go."

## 16

Of the twenty minutes spent edging his way back down to the first floor of the hospital, clinging to the banister for balance, Mike Hughes remembered very little. A bitter charcoal-drip in the back of his throat, one untied shoelace, the dirty steps: a patchwork of impressions that didn't add up. The only experience he could compare it with was the time he'd had pneumonia when he was nine and run a fever so high that his father had taken him out into the subzero winter night to drop his temperature.

*It's that smoke,* he thought, descending the last flight of stairs to the first floor. His head was pounding so hard it felt like it was going to burst, and he had to stop every few minutes to gag and retch until his empty stomach could only dry heave. The smoke had been oily, acrid, and it clung like tar to the inside of his mucous membranes. No amount of coughing and spitting was going to dislodge the taste.

And there were other things to think about.

Snow, for instance.

Snow was out.

Mike did not know how he was so sure of this, only that it had to be true. Looping the recent series of events through his mind only confirmed it. Walker and Calhoun had whisked Snow into the room at the end of the hall, looking for a vent to open his airway, and that explosion—if that's what it was—

Some kind of bomb? Had Snow smuggled something in, blown a hole in the wall, and escaped that way?

Impossible. Snow had looked weak, far too incapacitated to stage an escape attempt. Mike had seen his share of seizures, and the one Snow had thrown on the stretcher was an Oscar-class performance. Even if he'd some-how been faking respiratory arrest in the elevator, he would never have been able to bring explosives into the hospital, not with five cops guarding him. And if he had managed to jerry-rig some kind of incendiary device in that hidden room, a tank of oxygen or some sort of chemical, there hadn't been time for him to use it. That door hadn't been closed more than a few minutes before the screaming started.

What did that leave him with, then? Some kind of random industrial acci-dent that none of them could've predicted? Had Snow gotten free with the devil's own luck?

Mike's breath caught in his throat. The image flashed through his mind of Snow lying on the table in the scan room, eyes like broken bottle shards look-ing up from the bars of the head coil. He hadn't looked sick then.

*Something's here.*

Another thought whipsawed through his mind, almost too fast to catch. Where were Sarah and Eli right now? Still in the hospital waiting for him?

*Find a phone and call her cell. Just to make sure.*

Would she even talk to him at this point?

After his first affair was discovered five years ago, Mike's father had given him his only piece of advice on the matter of infidelity. *She might say she for-gives you, Mike, and if she does, then you need to take her at her word. But don't ever ex-pect her to forget, and don't be surprised if someday she takes the kid and leaves for good.*

*Yeah, but now?*

He was standing in the stairwell doorway, facing the long, empty corridor that ran past the emergency room to the main lobby and admissions and, if he followed it far enough, the chapel, which Calhoun had once told him was the oldest part of the entire building. The chapel was the only remaining part of the original structure, put up back in 1887. The building would close to-morrow, and Mike had never even gone back there.

Slowly, like a man who'd realized he'd ventured too deep into the woods and lost his way, he turned and looked in the other direction, toward the gift shop and the cafeteria. He knew this place, had logged hundreds of hours here, day and night. But this was different. Right now the emptiness was ab-solute, almost surreal. He thought for no good reason of the vacation he and

Sarah had taken to Germany six years ago, when they'd taken a bus trip to Dachau: the wide white walls and empty rooms, the endless corridors and gaping ovens.

It was as if something terrible had happened inside this place, too, something so horrific that every living thing had taken flight. The heavy sheets of plywood that had been nailed up over the windows only reinforced the feeling of isolation. For the first time it occurred to him that the perfect silence of it was eerie.

*Don't start that shit now, Mikey. You do not need it right now, trust me.*

"Find a phone," he said aloud, and though he wouldn't have admitted it, even the sound of his own voice was a comfort. "Just find a phone, call her, and pray she answers . . ."

*Because you're an asshole and you don't deserve her. Does Hallmark make a card that says that?*

Moving swiftly up the hall, he passed the east elevators and the door leading to the ER off to his left. It had never occurred to him to take the elevator down from the sixth floor. He'd always been told to avoid them in case of a fire—plus there was that brief but bizarre power failure in the elevator on their way up.

*Ought to try that ER door,* he thought. *Just to make sure it's still open.*

But that was crazy, too. Why wouldn't the ER entrance be open? It was the only way in or out of the hospital now. Nobody would've locked it down, unless—

Unless they wanted to keep Snow from escaping.

He cut left, through a set of double doors, leaving the main concourse and entering the ER. The silence felt deeper here, heralding an admixture of isolation and despair. Empty rooms had their own unnatural spaciousness, but they looked particularly bare with half the equipment removed. The paint inside had become dingy gray, peeling, like corpses' skin, under the fluorescent lights. In the corner of his eye he caught a glimpse of one of the room's floors, and it looked filthy with dried brownish footprints, as if someone had shuffled a drunken two-step through an immense pool of their own blood.

Up ahead was the ER nurses' station, where no phones rang and nothing moved. Mike walked faster, wanting to put that behind him. He was aware of his shoes squeaking on the floor, his breath quickening in his lungs, and for the first time he felt a sensation of heaviness looming over his shoulder.

Someone was watching him.

He stopped, jerked his head around, and looked back up the long, vacant hall. On either side, the doors of the ER rooms gaped stupidly open. Overhead, one of the light tubes flickered and went out. He held his breath. Nothing stirred; nothing made a sound. Yet the feeling of being watched had only grown more intense, less a sensation and more a certainty.

His heart was hammering, and not just because of his fast hustle down the hall. He swallowed, and had to do it three times before finding enough moisture to lubricate the back of his throat. He knew it now, right in his nerve endings: Snow *was* following him. He'd followed him down from upstairs, and he was hiding in one of the rooms, just out of view.

Panic swelled in his throat, and he stuffed it down.

*Don't panic. Stay cool. Just get out of here. You can call Sarah once you get outside.*

Up ahead, some thirty paces in front of him, he saw the steel door where Calhoun had let him in not even two hours earlier. Alongside it to the right was the ER waiting room, where you could normally look out at the rotunda where the ambulances picked up and dropped off, but that was all dark now, the fishbowl windows shuttered by big sheets of plywood. The only light came from the overhead fixtures.

Walking swiftly, not quite running, Mike cut the distance between himself and the door down to twenty feet, ten feet, five, and then he was there, both hands gripping the metal bar that would unlatch the steel door and release him into the open air of the early July evening. He pushed it.

The door didn't open.

He pushed the bar again, harder. It didn't budge. Even as he shoved it down and threw his hip against it, he knew the truth. The door wasn't stuck. It wasn't rusty. The hasp wasn't catching on something inside the jamb.

The door was locked.

Standing in front of it, still grasping the bar in his hands, he experienced the swimmy sensation of the unthinkable becoming the inevitable. Some part of him had known all along that the door would be locked, but his conscious mind, that well-intentioned housemother, had elected to spare him the unpleasantness. It was probably the last thought a chronic drunk driver had as his car veered across the double yellow into the oncoming lights of a semi: *Of course, this is how it has to end.*

Behind him, the soft rustle of footsteps.

Mike spun on his tiptoes with a startled squeak. Terror sent the copper taste through his mouth and sandbagged his belly. The sound had been very close, but he saw nothing, only the empty nurses' station and the empty hallway, the empty rooms and the fluttering overhead lights.

Something nearby had moved, stealthily but not that stealthily, as if it wanted him to hear it.

In the space of a heartbeat, he scanned his surroundings for possible weapons. His eyes fell on a steel IV pole lying on the floor and he grabbed it, backing away slowly from the direction he'd heard the footsteps.

He couldn't stay here. Two possibilities: the hall going to the right of the nurses' station, straight back to the main concourse; and the more indirect one to the left, back through the ER, the way he'd come. Either way he knew he had to pick a direction and go for it, *run*, had to abandon the false comfort of the door. The door was just another wall now, like all the other walls that surrounded him here, holding him in.

A hand grazed his hip, featherlight.

Mike's entire body jerked with a galvanic shrug and he flung himself forward in the opposite direction as if fired from a cannon, pumping his arms, pounding his feet, running up the hall to the left so fast that his body felt weightless, insubstantial, lighter than air.

He hit the doors to the main concourse without breaking stride, crashing through them and hooking right again. The IV pole in his hand caught on the doorjamb and he left it there, sprinting to the far end of the corridor, all the way to the west stairwell.

He didn't stop running until he opened the door to the stairs and pulled it shut behind him. Pressed to the wall, he was suddenly acutely aware of the peculiarity of his own flesh pulled tight over muscle and sinew. His lips felt numb, eyes glassine, unable to blink. The fear was fully disorienting, like the first taste of some ancient alcohol, an overwhelming spirit whose elemental effect on his species had not changed for thousands of years.

*Safe here,* Mike told himself, surprised that the words brought him any comfort at all. *I didn't hear it come after me, whatever it was, it didn't follow me here, I shut the door behind me—*

Gradually, his pulse and breathing began to normalize. The oxygen brought a welcome sense of levelheadedness, and he was relaxing into his first deep breath when the lights shuddered and went out.

# 17.

"Don't look," Sarah murmured to Eli, pushing his head down into her breast as she started through the door. "Close your eyes, don't look, just keep your—"

And stopped. Her hand crawled to cover her mouth, barely stifling the faint little moan of horror that escaped her lips. Though she couldn't have spent more than a moment or two looking at the scene sprawled out below her, it burned itself into her mind so deeply that she felt as if she'd been staring at it for hours.

Blood seemed to have been piped across the walls and ceiling with a high-pressure hose, sprayed in looping, dripping patterns in every direction. Within it all lay slabs and lumps like leftovers from some glutinous feast. Something eager and carnivorous had gorged itself here, ripping and slashing, digging out the tasty bits and leaving indiscriminate heaps of grayish-pink offal where they fell. Only moments later did Sarah realize that the pieces had once been a man.

On the top step, McPhee's severed arm lay crooked, still half-swathed in the soaked sleeve of his uniform, only two fingers, pinkie and thumb, jutting like bits of crabmeat from the mangled blob of flesh that had been his hand. Gobbets of muscle and tendon dangled listlessly from denuded bone. Two steps below that, a pale haunch of something tufted with fine black hairs lay shimmering in an already coagulating pool of blood, a scrap of undershirt draped over it, saturated in deep, arterial red. Sarah's mind flashed back to when her dad and her brother, Terry, used to take her fishing out at Crystal Lake and afterward they'd gut the bluegills and sunfish, leaving dinner for the gulls. Her stomach gave an audible lurch and she gagged, throwing up a little into her mouth.

"Mommy?" Fear in Eli's voice now, his face lifting from the swell of her chest. "What—"

Still trying to swallow, Sarah grabbed his head and shoved it back against her. She prayed that the boy didn't see this, prayed that he kept his eyes closed. Finally, she turned her head and spat without looking at the floor. "Don't you look," she croaked, and coughed until her throat was clear. "You keep your head down and eyes closed and don't look until I say, do you understand?"

"Yes, Mommy."

At the bottom of the stairs, she saw McPhee's head, upturned, mouth and eyes open in an expression of eternal astonishment. She was going to have to step over it to get her keys. Could she do that?

No way.

But if she didn't . . .

Steeling herself, she started making her way down the stairs, among the parts, choosing each step with trembling, painstaking care. She could count how many steps were left until she was past it: twelve, perhaps less, but she didn't want to overstep, to slip and—

The lights went out.

Sarah froze, the darkness crowding in on her like the dirt of a premature burial, constricting her throat until she couldn't breathe. Eyes blind, the vision lingered in her mind, the last thing she'd glimpsed before the blackout, a subliminal flash of something moving in front of her.

Eli's hands pinched her closer.

"Mommy," his voice whispered, "what's going on?"

She couldn't speak.

"Mommy?"

Say something, for God's sake.

"The power's out."

"Why?"

"I don't know."

"Did that man do it?"

"I don't know, honey."

She knew that it was her job as a parent to whisper reassurances to him, to tell him that everything was going to be all right. But at the moment, in such darkness, she didn't trust herself to formulate those familiar old nostrums.

*Turn. Just turn around. You have the railing. It's right here . . .*

But for one dreadful moment her hand was so hot and numb she wasn't sure she *could* feel the railing anymore. Her other arm, locked around Eli, seemed to have absorbed all the feeling from her body. Her fingers groped and slapped upward until yes, there it was, and she clutched it, jerking herself around and upward, upward, toward where she knew the door must be.

## 18

The power outage happened over a span of perhaps three seconds, the lights overhead dimming, sputtering, and then disappearing completely, burying Mike in a wave of blackness that passed through the entire hospital like the last gasp of a dying man.

He held his hand in front of his face and saw nothing. The tidal wave of disorientation was immediate and multisensory. All at once the stairwell, normally so familiar to his eyes, became some vast and unknown cave. His fingers groped and met the cement wall behind him, tracing the grooves between the cinder blocks. It felt cool, almost moist, in the dark.

*What's happening here?*

*Snow. He cut the power. And the backup generators, too.*

*Why? How?*

But he knew the answer to that, too, didn't he? At least the first part. Not logically, maybe, but on a deeper level, where truth bypassed the forebrain and went straight to the nerve endings. It took only a moment in the dark for the entirety of Snow's purpose to take shape, the way the glow-in-the-dark constellations that Mike had glued to Eli's bedroom ceiling would crystallize seconds after he switched off the light.

*He's hunting us.*

The darkness was getting to him already, finding his weak points and snipping them like strings. It made him think about whatever it was that had grazed past him, back in the ER, on its way—

"Snow," he murmured. "It was Snow, so why don't you just call it that?"

*What if he reached out for me now, here in the dark? What would I do? Where would I run?*

Hysteria brushed close against him then, sleek as mink, leaving him momentarily ready to scream. Mike bit his lip until salty blood drifted over the tip of his tongue and his whole mouth throbbed. It helped, a little, but never in his life had he felt so confused and helpless, so absolutely broken in half by fear.

He took a deep breath and let it out. There was a flashlight in one of the drawers down in MRI. He knew exactly where it was; he'd put it there himself, more than a year ago.

He reached back and found the wall again. Inching to his left, his foot ventured toward where he knew the edge of the first step would be. It was there, as was the railing. Mike lowered himself down. With the railing in hand it became easier to move forward, and he fumbled down the next six steps without incident, finding himself on the landing. If he turned ninety degrees and reached out with his right hand, he could follow the next dozen or so steps to the ground floor. From there he could feel his way down the hall to the MRI control room, to the drawer beneath the microwave, and when he got the flashlight he would reevaluate his options. He would—

Below him, in the darkness, something shifted.

Mike froze, clutching the railing, his eyes helplessly held wide against the blackness. His heart was booming in his ears like far-off artillery. The big ventilation fans had all stopped when the power went out, and the stairwell was quieter than he'd ever heard it.

*Something moved down there. I know it.*

He tried to think of what kind of noise it had been. A shuffling sound, like a shoe scraping? Or was it the rustle of fabric? Or a cough? Sarah would've known.

Now there was nothing.

Mike held his breath. He could almost feel his auditory canals reaching out to search the darkness like long antennae and coming back empty.

But he would have to walk through that nothing to get to where he was going.

*Ask yourself this: How certain are you that you even heard something in the first place?*

In the end it didn't matter. He could stand here forever. There was only one light source in this entire hospital whose location he was absolutely sure of, and to get it, he'd have to go straight down those stairs.

*Count to sixty. If you haven't heard anything by then, go ahead.*

He started to count. It didn't take as long as he'd thought, so he kept counting until he reached a hundred. And then two hundred. Still no sound.

For the first time his mind opened itself to the possibility that he really *could* have imagined the noise, or if not, it might have had a perfectly normal explanation, a creaky pipe, an old foundation, some mundane sound he would never have noticed under normal circumstances. He found he'd begun to visualize the bottom of the stairs with no one there—no one had been there to begin with.

He started moving again, easing down the steps like a man wading into very cold water, one shuffling step, and then the next. Every few seconds his chest would start aching and he realized he was forgetting to breathe.

*Here's where I feel the hand grab me. Or the knife slides into my spine. Right now. Here's where the fingers take hold of my throat—*

With mammoth effort, he extended his hand as far into the darkness as it would go, reaching out and down until he felt the door, applying pressure until it opened with an awful, disruptive squawk.

He stepped through. The dark felt cooler here. Mike put out his arm and moved it to the right until he felt the wall of the ground floor. Flattening himself against it, he crept forward in those same slow and silent steps. His throat felt as if someone had reached down and swabbed every drop of moisture from it.

Up and to the right, he brushed against a hard-edged shape protruding from the wall at face level. One finger traced the edge of what was engraved there and slowly he recognized the letter *M.*

And beside it, *R.*

And then *I.*

He found the door handle, cold in the dark, and twisted it open. This time the hinges were silent, as he'd known they would be. He oiled them himself, spraying them regularly with a can of WD-40 kept under the sink. He had expected that silence would make him feel better but it didn't.

The little waiting area could not have been more than fifteen feet to the other side. Trying to envision it in his mind, Mike strode quickly across, his panic gnawing through the compartment in his mind where he'd managed to contain it up until now. He began flailing his hands for the inner door, the one going into the MRI suite, seizing the knob and yanking it, knocking over a chair. It fell with a crash and his face went numb with dread.

"Fuck," he said. "Oh, fuck." Now everything in the darkness sounded too loud. He spun around, heard papers shuffling under his feet, something tinkling, and plunged both hands into absolute blackness until they bumped off the counter. Here was the cold metal of the sink, a pile of Tupperware clattering down, the microwave, until he felt the drawer. Mike pulled it open.

*The flashlight won't be here. After all this, it won't—*

But of course it was, and he found its shape almost immediately with both hands and switched it on. A strong and solid bar of light shone across the room in front of him and Mike heard himself exhale with relief so deep it seemed to come from his toes upward.

He shined the light deep into the block of empty space. Seeing that the suite truly was empty, that Frank Snow was not down here waiting for him with a scalpel or a bone saw, Mike felt himself becoming calmer, becoming more himself again.

He took a step forward and stopped cold.

To his immediate right, resting on the floor amid the pile of papers that he'd just kicked over, was a cell phone and a brown leather key chain. Mike recognized both instantly. He'd bought the key chain for Sarah for their first anniversary, when she'd jokingly asked for a Coach bag that she knew they couldn't afford. Mike had wrapped it up in a big box and given it to her, and they'd laughed and made love all that night.

Her car keys were still attached to it.

## 19

Only when Sarah was once again back in the main lobby, with tortuous slowness, did her eyes began to adjust. Somewhere not far away, she realized, light was trickling into the darkness. The darkness devoured it hungrily but not entirely, leaving a faint haze of thirdhand illumination she could see only because of the black totality surrounding it.

She carried her son toward the waning ghost of late evening light. In the ER waiting room the last threads of the twilight were trickling between the cracks of the boards nailed over the windows. She could just make out the first set of doors leading to the ER exit.

Though her arms were starting to get tired from carrying Eli, she held him even closer as she approached the door and pushed on it. It didn't move. She pushed again. Locked.

*But that's impossible. If it's locked . . . if there's no way out . . .*

She thought of the jingling keys she'd heard earlier. Whoever it was had locked them in. She knew who it was, but couldn't bring herself to think his name.

Around her the room turned black.

Eli squirmed in her arms, wiggling one hand down into her purse. A moment later she saw something flickering between his fingers. Its faint glow felt somehow vast and powerful. Sarah stared at it.

"Honey, what is that?"

"The Express," he said. "It will help us find Daddy."

"Can I see it?"

He handed over the little toy train with the miniature lightbulb, willing as always to share his toys with any adult who showed the slightest interest. She held the Express out, peering through its tiny brightness. She thought of downstairs, car keys no use to her now if they were locked in, but—

What about her cell phone? She groped in her purse but couldn't find it. Had she left that downstairs, too? The cell reception from the hospital was notoriously terrible, but she had to try. She didn't have a choice.

The man who had locked them in had gone the other way, away from the doorway through which he'd come. Hiding behind the information desk with Eli, listening to the diminishing sound of the keys, Sarah had as much as heard it as seen it. She'd seen it with her ears.

"Where are we going, Mommy?"

"Back down." She drew in a breath, feeling her resolve strengthen. "So we can call for help."

# 20.

Fists throbbing, out of breath, Steve Calhoun took a single uncertain step backward through the ER waiting room, the lines on his face etched by the cigarette glowing from his lips. He paused to look down at his scraped knuckles but could only make out a pair of pale blobs, blobs that should've been holding his keys.

*Clumsy. Stupid. Just like your father.*

After concealing himself in a supply closet on one of the upper floors, hoping that Snow would just get his freakish escape over with and flee the hospital so that life could go back to normal, Calhoun had finally decided that it was time to leave his hiding place when the power went out. Coming down and finding the ER entrance locked, he had spent the last ten minutes pounding on the plywood sheets that the workmen had nailed over the windows. At first it had seemed like an easy enough thing to knock the plywood loose—it was, after all, only plywood—but that didn't turn out to be the case. He'd tried kicking, punching, and ramming his shoulder into it, and it didn't budge. Now he was considering picking up some heavy object, one of the end tables full of magazines, maybe, or a wheelchair, and throwing it through. Even if it didn't work, throwing something would feel damn good.

*You don't deserve to feel good. You lost your keys. You'd lose your own head if it weren't attached, you stupid, clumsy—*

"Shut up, Ma," Calhoun muttered, unaware that he was even talking out loud. "Just shut up, okay?"

*Just like he was. Woozy with booze. All those bottles at the end of every week and the trashmen would stand there shaking their heads, laughing—*

He felt nauseated, feverish. *What you saw up there must have done this to you,*

*Steve.* When that door had slammed shut behind him and Walker and Frank Snow, and Calhoun had looked down and seen . . . seen . . .

He let his gaze stray off into the dark, as if there might be a place he could look and not see that other room exactly as it had been. In the end smoke had blackened everything, blinding him, and he only wished it had come sooner, much sooner.

It had been some kind of children's hospital room. There was a little bed inside and a little table and chair and some old toys on the floor that nobody had played with for a long time. Calhoun remembered a yellow duck on a string, sticking halfway out from underneath the bed. They had rolled Snow's stretcher in and Dr. Walker had started speaking all weird, saying words that hadn't made any sense. He'd only gotten a few of those words out when Snow had—

*—sat up straight on that stretcher with his eyes wide open and that grin ripping across his face, and it happened so fast—*

But the speed of the initial events hadn't really interfered with Calhoun's recall. If anything they'd only seared the salient details more deeply into his brain. He remembered how he'd backed up and knocked something over behind him, probably that tray of tools, and when he'd looked up again, Dr. Walker had gone pale and still.

What had happened next in that children's hospital room, what Steve Calhoun had seen before the smoke blocked it out, he never intended to speak of to anyone. Partly because he couldn't believe it himself, but mainly because he was afraid.

*What, that actually happened? You saw those things?*

He sucked harder on the cigarette, brightening its tip from orange to a lurid cherry-red.

Then he stopped.

Across the room, twenty feet away, another orange light floated in the dark.

"Shit!" Calhoun said and jumped bolt upright, his own cigarette almost falling from his lips. His eyes fixed on the glowing cherry. Someone else was standing here in the dark, smoking and watching him.

*Unless—*

Slowly, he brought his hand up and took the cigarette from his mouth, lowering it. The other orange speck obediently followed suit. Calhoun raised his cigarette again. The other speck came up.

Ah.

He almost chuckled at his own foolishness. It was his own reflection he was seeing, shining off something, a sheet of glass or some polished surface in the dark waiting room. He brought the cigarette back to his lips and the orange speck did the same. *Nerves,* he thought again, shakily, and started to inhale. *Fucking nerves are running away from me.*

Not just nerves, drinking, too. In fact, when he got out of here, he was going to start making a real effort to get his ass to a meeting and—

The other orange speck went back down again, all by itself.

Calhoun stopped breathing, not a conscious decision. His breath simply stopped.

Instinct sprang though him and he turned and fled. He kept his hands out in front of him like a sleepwalker, flipping and thumping off the unseen landscape of chairs, angles, and edges, his breathing fast and shallow, his feet staggering. A jingling sound followed him. At least once it sounded so close that he thought Snow was walking alongside him in the blackness, dangling the keys next to his ear. Head down, Calhoun blundered left, into what he hoped was a corridor of private ER rooms.

*A door, I know there's a door here, one that I can shut—*

Turning left again, he felt the outer jamb of a door that he could hopefully close and reinforce from the inside. Barricading himself in again was a sucker bet but he was out of options. He jumped in and slammed the door closed behind him and put his back to it, shot one hand into his pocket, and gripped his lighter with trembling, sweating hands. His thumb rested on the little wheel. His lungs were screaming.

*What if I flick it and the light comes up and I see him in here grinning at me? Grinning that same grin he had when he—*

His thumb twitched and scratched the lighter's wheel to life.

The flame threw light across the room in agonizing gradations, Calhoun's eyes swelling to take everything in at once. A severed umbilicus of braided wires dangled from the wall. A bag of dirty linen lay next to his feet in a pool of dark, dried liquid. Beyond that there was nothing else in here, nothing but him.

He sank to the floor next to the laundry bag, shaking and gulping air, his back still to the door. He listened for the jingling sound, but now all he heard, from the far side of that door, was soft, congested-sounding laughter.

Within a moment, that, too, was gone.

## 21

Back on the stairwell going down, Sarah finally had to bring herself to step over the rest of McPhee.

The yellow-orange cone of the Express's headlight was just enough to out-line the step in front of them, to keep her from falling. It was also enough to see his blood shining on the walls, hanging there in half-dried sheets. And the slick, lymphatic edgelessness of his staring head.

*Don't look.* She pulled Eli's head against her neck, made him keep his eyes shut.

"Is it okay, Mommy?"

"Hush, honey. Let Mommy listen." The soles of her shoes made gummy sounds. She got to the landing, halfway down. Something crooked and three-dimensional lay tucked in the deep shadows, mercifully obscured, but when the tip of her foot struck some part of it she hadn't noticed, it was all she could do to keep from crying out.

*Don't look. Don't look. Just keep going.*

Sarah took her sense of sight out of the equation, instead focusing every-thing on her ears, attuned to all the far-off creaks and gurgles that the build-ing made around her as she crept down the last few steps to the ground level. It was hard to tell the sounds from their echoes, reverberations that described immensity, emptiness, size, vacuity.

Another step. And one more.

Now she aimed the Express downward, allowing herself to look again. No blood this far down, no soft, broken shapes, the floor clean.

She pushed the door open to the ground floor. This was how they'd come down before from their entrance on the first floor, but everything was different now, distances stretched, swimming in near blackness.

"Mommy, can I look now?"

Sarah nodded, was about to say, *Go ahead, you won't see much,* when she heard the speaker crackling up somewhere in front of them.

She froze, the boy clutching her shoulder.

"What's that, Mommy?"

"A radio, sounds like." The noise she heard was primarily composed of static, with an occasional chirp or flutter of electronic feedback. It sounded far away, she thought, but then didn't *everything* sound far away in the darkness?

There was another muted cloud of static, and Sarah heard a voice crackling through the speaker, saying, "Unit Six, do you copy?"

Sarah squinted ahead, holding the toy engine slightly higher as she made dubious progress. The arm she was using to carry Eli had long ago stopped aching and was now numb and trembling with fatigue, but she couldn't quite bring herself to put him down. Not with the darkness so close, rubbing up against them like a thick fog.

"Unit Six?" the radio voice said. "Confirm position."

Up ahead on the left Sarah could make out the outline of a door. She raised the Express. No sign here. She put her hand on the knob, prepping for it to be locked. But it turned easily in her hand.

"Mommy?" Eli whispered. "Can I hold my train for a little?"

She realized the comfort that she'd been denying him, clutching his toy for as long as she had; yet she was surprised at how difficult it was to relinquish. "Here, hold it up so we can see inside," she whispered back, and without another word Eli took the Express, let go of her neck, and slipped down to stand on his own. As much as she didn't want to let him go, her right arm sighed with relief. "You have to stay right next to me, understand? Do not let go of my hand."

"Okay."

She nudged the door open just a few inches, cocking her head to listen. She didn't have to wait long.

The radio sounds were appreciably louder on the other side of the door, a good sign, maybe. "Hello?" Realizing no one could hear her unless she at least risked speaking in normal room volume, she spoke louder. "Is someone here?"

In the dark Eli was right next to her, clutching her hand and holding the train dutifully up over his head to shed its faint illumination. The first room they entered was stacked with boxes, some wooden crates, some cardboard packing. Everything wore a thick, greasy layer of dust. There was an entire box of old telephones, their receivers tangled hopelessly in a snake pit of coiled cords. Another box held hundreds of pairs of old eyeglasses. A third, smaller box was full of tiny, putty-colored objects that she realized were hearing aids. Sarah lifted her gaze, and what she saw next brought a sharp squawk of fright to the very cusp of her lips. She yanked Eli up alongside her where she could cover him with both arms.

"Ow, Mommy, you're hurting me! You're—"

His voice broke off as he saw where she was looking. Hanging from hooks above the boxes was a row of small bodies. Their arms and legs dangled limply, heads angled toward the floor, eyes and mouths gaping open. White X's had been painted broadly across their tiny breastbones.

She looked at the blank eyes, the open mouths. They were pediatric mannequins, she realized—dummies used to teach CPR. To their left, she made out the silhouettes of adult dummies suspended from hooks of their own, the figures masked in darkness.

Dull relief dropped into her stomach, and she breathed again, temples throbbing. She crossed the room to the door opposite her, where the radio crackling was louder still, and it occurred to her that Frank Snow might be in there with a police radio, that maybe he had taken it from McPhee. He would be standing in the darkness just beyond that door, waiting for her.

The tiny train light disappeared, Eli's fingers slipping from her hand.

"Eli?" For the second time in as many minutes, fear found her throat and squeezed. "*Eli?* Where are you?"

Thirty seconds later, she heard his voice up ahead, near where the radio noise was coming from. And not just his voice. Someone was speaking to her son through the radio.

The train light floated ten feet in front of her. His small face appeared beside it like a half-moon. "It's okay, Mommy. The door's open."

"Get back here."

"But—"

"Now!" she ordered, panic making her voice harsher than necessary, and as the light bobbed dutifully toward her, the radio noise came with it. Eli was holding the walkie-talkie in his left hand, frowning at it.

"Where did you get that?"

"I found it through there," he said, pointing through the open doorway. "I was trying to tell you—"

"Let me see it, please." She took the radio, fumbling with the knobs. "And the Express, too."

Eli handed it over with a sigh. Sarah squatted down so that she could wedge the walkie-talkie between her knees and hold the train light close by, freeing up her right hand to decipher the half-dozen knobs that sprouted alongside the rubberized antenna.

Eli pointed. "You press that button to talk."

"How do you know that?"

"He told me."

"Who were you talking to?"

"A policeman. He talked first."

"What did he say?"

"He told me which button to push to talk and I did it."

"What did you tell him?"

"He wanted to know our names so I said your names, Mike and Sarah Hughes, so he knows who we are."

Holding the Express as close as she could to the radio, Sarah pushed the "talk" button and brought the device to her mouth. "Hello? Is anyone there? Hello, this is an emergency, can anyone hear me?"

There was a long silence, then a voice said, "Hello, is this Sarah?"

"Yes." She gripped the radio more tightly. "Who is this?"

"I think you know me."

She couldn't respond, couldn't move.

"You're wondering what I want," he said. "Don't worry. I'm not here to take anything from you. Certainly nothing you won't bring to me of your own free will before the night's over." This possibility seemed to amuse him greatly. "Now Sarah, let's talk about what I can do for you."

Sarah felt the dark room expanding around her in all directions. She still couldn't speak, lost in the void that had swallowed her life.

She forced herself to breath and finally found her voice. "Please, just let us go."

"Done. Anything else?"

"What?"

"I asked if that was all you wanted."

"Yes," she said. "That's all."

"It won't be a problem at all," he said. "When the time comes, all you'll have to do is follow the signs."

## 22

Flashlight under his arm, Mike couldn't tell how long he stood perfectly still, holding Sarah's keys in his hand. Here was the Coach tag, the Outback's clicker, her house keys, and her membership tags for Sam's Club, CVS, and Blockbuster. Within this context they felt talismanic, mundane objects infused with supernatural powers.

*Maybe they got away anyway,* a voice within him gibbered. *Maybe they got out and walked away, ran away, maybe somebody gave them a ride, maybe—*

The flashlight caught another object from her bag, a crumpled note on the floor. Mike picked it up, saw Jolie's handwriting:

> *M:*
> *Friday will be our last night together. This calls for a celebration, don't you*
> *think? I'll bring the champagne.*
> *J.*

He stared at it for a long moment, almost forgetting where he was and why. He heard Sarah saying, *I found this in your pocket last night* as she dumped everything on the floor. Only now did he realize Jolie's note must have been what brought his wife here in the first place.

He picked up her cell phone, switched it on. The screen blinked NO SERVICE, a dark confirmation of the worst. His wife and son, here because of his own foolishness, were still locked inside the hospital. There was no getting around it, out of it, through it. Everything that had happened up until now was his fault entirely.

*And Walker's. What was Walker—*

"Daddy?"

Mike stiffened. From somewhere, unbelievable but unmistakable, came the voice of his son. Then, as if to confirm what his mind could not quite accept, he heard it again, louder:

"*Mike?*"

He sucked in a breath, gasped as if somebody had punched him hard in the gut. Then he turned, dropped the keys and cell phone, and ran. Eli's cry was still ringing in his ears as he burst out into the hallway, the flashlight's pale oval jigging and flying along the far wall like a bouncing ball in an old-time movie house sing-along. He supposed it was stupid, no, *knew* it was stupid, putting himself out in the open like this, but he couldn't have stopped if he wanted to. *When you trip, you fall down; when your son cries out from the darkness, you come running, because—*

"Eli!" he bellowed, voice ringing hugely down the hall. *"It's daddy! Where are you?"* He spun around, aimed the flashlight the other way. The hall was quiet now, empty. "Eli?"

At the far end of the corridor Mike saw a large soiled linen cart parked at the corner. It was one of the industrial-sized carts that normally held four hundred pounds of bagged sheets and towels: as big as a small garbage Dumpster, and Mike was fairly certain that it hadn't been there earlier, when he'd talked to Dr. Walker by the coffee machine.

*No, you're positive it wasn't, and you know it.*

Worse, something about the way the linen cart sat there made it look as if someone had just pushed it around the corner a moment before his arrival. The flashlight beam reflected off a pool of something dripping through the bottom of the cart. Mike imagined he could hear the faint *plip . . . plip . . . plip* of droplets echoing through the long open hall.

What he didn't have to imagine was the sound of his son's voice. It was coming from inside the cart.

"Daddy? *Mike?*"

Mike started forward.

It wasn't long before he could see things sticking up out of the top. One of those things was a human hand. Another was a foot with a shoe still attached to it. The shoe was brown and worn down at the heel. Now the dripping sound was not just in his imagination; he could hear it with agonizing clarity.

*Plip . . . plip . . . plip.*

There were four bodies stuffed into the cart. Mike saw blue uniforms, soaked black. Inside it the police officers were packed together, one upside-down, two mashed face-to-face, like some hideous cartoon parody of commuters on a rush-hour subway car. One of them, who looked like the big cop, Oz, stared out at him flat-eyed, mouth slightly agape.

Static burst from the radio clipped to the cop's belt, and from the speaker, Mike heard his son's voice blasting out at high volume: "Daddy . . . *Mike* . . ."

Mike grabbed the radio, pulled it free, and keyed the mic. "Eli, it's Daddy. Can you hear me?"

"Daddy . . . *Mike* . . ."

"Where are you, honey?"

". . . Mommy . . . Sarah Hughes . . . Daddy . . ."

Mike almost hit the "talk" button again and stopped, listening to Eli's voice coming from the dead cop's walkie-talkie.

"Daddy . . . *Mike* . . ."

Not his son, not live, anyway: a recording. Eli wasn't speaking to him at all. He was simply answering questions, repeating his parents' names to some unseen interlocutor. And whoever was on the other end of the police radio was simply playing that taped message over . . . and over . . . and over—

Mike held the radio in the flashlight's beam and pushed the button.

"Who is this?"

"Daddy . . . *Mike* . . ."

*Who are you kidding? You're not going to hear anything more than the recording. That's all it is. You're wasting your time.*

"Hello?"

Now even the recording had given way to dead air. A cramp of near hysteria cut through his body, piercing his lungs.

"Hello, Lover Boy," the speaker said.

Mike stared at the radio, the flashlight beam trembling.

"Got your number, don't I?" The voice was playful, whimsical, but with an edge. "Couldn't wait to send your wife and child away tonight so you and that nasty piece of tail of yours could get up to the devil's business, isn't that a fact?"

Mike swallowed. Now he felt punched in the throat.

"Only problem is, Mike, I come here tonight on the devil's true business."

"Please." He realized he wasn't holding the button down. He pushed it and said again, "Please, don't kill them."

"Kill them? Who, your pretty wife and child?" Snow asked. "That's not a bad idea. I guess I wouldn't mind seeing what they look like flayed open all nice and smooth. But I'm here to make a deal."

"Then make your deal with me instead. I'll do whatever you want."

"We already made one deal, remember? I'm glad you decided to stay and party, instead of being a bore and leaving." Mike thought of the note that Snow had passed him earlier, back in the MRI suite. "But don't worry, Lover Boy. I like you. When the time comes, I might even give you a chance to make another choice, a courtesy I don't extend often."

"Please. Just tell me what I need to do." He took his finger off the button, waited. Static crackled, then a different voice:

"Daddy . . . *Mike* . . ."

The recording again. The radio fell to the floor—dropped more than thrown—and Mike shined the flashlight up the hall. Nothing to see there. On legs that felt stilted and mechanical, he went back through the waiting room into the MRI suite. Squatting down under the computer console, he groped around for a moment until he found the aluminum bat that Repko had asked about earlier.

He returned to the hallway, holding the bat in one hand and clutching the flashlight with the other. Somewhere something fell, crashed, not too far away but still overly loud to his ears. The size of the hallways, their sheer depth and vacancy, amplified the most delicate noises into the sound of thunder.

Out of nowhere a Bradbury line occurred to him, stuck in his mind from a junior high paper he'd once written on *Something Wicked This Way Comes*: "They eat the dark, who only stand and breathe."

*Eat the dark*, yes, that was all he could do. Anything could be hiding wherever it pleased, anything with enough patience and appetite, clutching itself in darkness and waiting.

Mike raised the flashlight and froze in his tracks with a grunt of surprise.

The linen cart with the bodies of the dead cops was now lying on its side. Three of the corpses were sprawled across the corridor, the radio next to them.

*Except there should be four.*

He played the flashlight over the bodies to the greasy smear of blood leading away from the upended cart and around the next corner.

There *had* been four of them. He knew it. So where was the fourth?

*Only problem is, Mike, I come here tonight on the devil's true business.*

All at once he heard the sound, not as far off as the crash he'd heard before. This one came from just around the corner, some bastard hybrid of a gurgle and a sob. He was still looking at the corner when the thing lunged around it at him.

He jerked the bat up but it was too late. The thing—the man—grabbed him by the shoulders, knocking him back, shaking the flashlight from his hands. In the darkness Mike could feel the other man's breath in his face. It smelled like hot salt and minerals, tinged with the odors of sweat and parts of the body never meant to be exposed to air.

"Did you see him?" the man demanded. "Where is he?"

Mike's throat opened but nothing came out. The speechlessness lasted long enough that he thought he'd been rendered permanently mute, the language center of his brain literally snuffed out by fright.

"You're one of the cops," he managed at last. "You were still *alive* in there?"

Somewhere off to his left, the flashlight came back up and the cop's face appeared in front of him. Not Repko or Oz, but one of the others. He realized the cop was holding a flashlight of his own, a better one. For a moment Mike thought he might be looking into a mirror reflecting his own terrorized face. Through the caked-on blood, the cop's wide-eyed expression slowly became one of comprehension, even relief.

"You're the MRI guy."

"You scared the shit out of me," Mike said.

The cop was staring at the bodies in blue uniforms, spilled across the floor. "That son of a bitch. We never saw him coming."

Mike nodded. "What happened?"

"I blacked out up on Six. Woke up facedown in that cart with my partners' bodies jammed against me so tight I could feel them getting stiff. *Fuck.*" He rubbed both hands over his face, pulling his eyes down until all Mike saw was pink.

Mike hesitated, not wanting to ask the question. He did anyway. "Snow didn't . . . give you guys a choice?"

The cop blinked. "A choice? What are you . . . wait. Holy shit. He told us on the way over that if we just dropped him off at the hospital and left, he'd let us live. Of course, we just laughed our asses off. Jesus, this is bad. We gotta roll. Now."

"My wife and son are still in here."

The cop blinked at him, his horror somehow stretching even farther into the outer reaches of his face. "In this hospital somewhere? With Snow?"

Mike nodded.

"How do you know?"

"I know. Plus I heard my son's voice." He pointed at the radio lying on the floor. "On that."

The cop picked up the radio and switched it on.

"Daddy . . . Mike . . ." Eli's voice said, and after a beat, "Mommy . . . Sarah Hughes . . ."

"What's he saying?"

"Our names, my wife's and mine. It's a recording. It just plays over and over."

"So how do you know he's still here?" The cop hardly paused to give Mike a chance to answer. "Doesn't matter. We still gotta find a way out first."

"Snow locked the doors, but there's a tunnel in the basement."

"Is it open?"

"I don't know."

"Then we're going upstairs to bust our way out. Through the doors, windows, whatever. That way at least one of us can get backup. Your boy's chances are better if he and your wife can just hide somewhere until we get more officers to search the building." The cop was already walking away from him. "Come on."

## 23

"Sarah? It *is* Sarah, isn't it?" Snow's voice asked from out of the walkie-talkie's speaker. "May I ask you something, Sarah?"

"What?"

"Where's your boy, Sarah? Where's little Eli?" Voice sloping down to a whisper: "Where's my boy meat?"

She spun around, clutching the ridiculous toy train.

*Eli was gone.*

At that same instant she realized she could smell something, an acrid rotten-egg odor that was turning the air to rubber cement in her nostrils.

*He's in here with me.*

*But that's impossible, that's—*

Without thinking, she charged forward, dropping the toy train and bolting headlong into absolute dark. Her left leg kicked something sharp and angular, and as she fell, she heard a box of small objects—the glasses, perhaps, or the hearing aids—go tinkling across the floor, skittering under the soles of her sneakers.

Then it was silent.

She was alone.

"Sarah?" the speaker crackled, from somewhere near her head. "You're still there, aren't you? I think you are. And I think you can hear *this* just fine."

"Mommy . . . ?" It was Eli's voice coming through the radio. "Sarah Hughes . . . ? Daddy?"

"Thing of it is, I'm watching him right now. He can't see me, but I can see him. He's lost, but I know exactly where he is. He's very nearby."

She reached out in the dark and found the radio. Pressed the button she'd pushed before. "Leave him alone. He didn't do anything. Let him go, don't hurt him."

"I'm not going to hurt him. I promise."

There was another long pause, and Snow said, "Eli, say hi to your mommy," and Sarah heard Eli's voice a third time, so close to the radio now that the sound distorted in a toneless blast of static. *"MOMMY? SARAH HUGHES?"*

"Leave him alone!" Sarah shouted. "Stop it!"

But she was talking to nothing.

## 24

Under no circumstances would Eli have left his mother's side—he knew all about candy and strangers, smiling, clean-shaven men who might even say they were friends of his mommy or daddy.

But while mommy was busy talking through the police radio, Eli was sure he had heard his father's voice shouting for him from down the hall. The sound of his daddy yelling his name had made him feel so good, so safe, that he hadn't thought twice about leaving his mother behind with the radio and running out into the corridor. Once he found his daddy, they could go back and get his mom again. His daddy would know what to do. His daddy always knew.

But now he was in a new hallway, without even the train's light to guide him, and his father was nowhere to be heard. He'd run so far that he was worried he could have passed his daddy in the dark. Worse, looking back, he didn't know which direction he'd come from, because he couldn't see.

"Daddy?" he whispered. And louder: "*Daddy?*" The gravity of his error settled over him and he felt scared tears climbing in his throat, making it feel sore and tight. "*Daddy . . . ?*"

In the long darkness that stretched out in front of him, Eli heard something beginning to stir. It was alive and making itself larger.

He ran blindly, without thought or destination, the same breath locked in his lungs that had been there for the last ten seconds. The only sound he made was a soft, high-pitched keening, an ultrasonic dog-whistle that escaped through his nose as his feet slapped the floor, rocketing him forward.

He hit a sharp object and bounced back, pain spiking his forehead and startling him back to clarity. Where was he? On the floor, still unable to see anything.

Reaching out, he felt a flat rectangular thing in front of him, the edge of an open door. Eli felt the cold crooked piece of metal that was the doorknob. Through the ringing in his ears, he could still hear movement behind him in the dark.

Crying, sobbing, too scared to think, he crawled through the opening, drew his knees up to his chin, wrapped his arms around his legs. There was a low shelf behind him with things stacked on it. Straightening his arms out, Eli gripped the end of the door and pulled it shut in front of him, and closed his eyes.

When he opened them again he was on the Island of Sodor.

It was a world he recognized instantly. All around him, a picture-postcard landscape of rolling hills and trees shone like emeralds in the mild sunlight. The sky was a generous swath of blue that seemed to go on forever. Gazing up the railway tracks, he saw the darker blue paint of Thomas the Tank Engine smiling as he came over the hill, great cheerful clouds of white cotton puffing from his funnel. His whistle *peep-peep*ed brightly as he hissed to a stop next to Eli, dumping off steam. Then his smile faded.

"There's trouble on the line, Eli. You'd better be careful. Driver says it's not safe to go out today."

Eli put his small hands up to touch the smooth globes of Thomas's cheeks. They were warm, just as he'd known they would be. "What should we do?"

"Stay here. Don't move."

"Is it . . ." Eli thought hard to remember the man's full name. "Is it Frank Snow?"

"Never mind who." Thomas's eyes rolled away, the remains of his cheerful expression darkening by degrees. "Just stay here and don't make a sound."

"Don't leave," Eli whispered. "Stay here with me."

Thomas gave a single *peep*. "Of course, I will."

"Promise?"

"An engine's word is as good as gold." Thomas attempted another smile, but as he did, Eli noticed something leaking from the corner of the engine's mouth. His expression had fallen slack on one side, his right eye sagging and sloping like candle wax. Without warning, an explosive burst of thick fluid spilled up from his boiler, trickling over his face, and when Thomas tried to speak again it came out in a clotted gargle of incomprehensible clucks, blurps, and growls. Eli understood that Thomas was sick, very sick, maybe dying, because of something on the other side of the door.

"What's wrong?"

"He's going to make a meal of you," the engine said, in his new, glutinous voice. Now his face appeared to be dissolving in a river of foul-smelling leakage pouring from his funnel. "Glork! Not safe! Driver says—"

The doorknob turned.

Eli clapped both hands over his mouth and squeezed as far back as he could under the low shelf above his head. The Shape on the other side had stopped, and Eli heard the door open in front of him.

*Stay here. Don't move.*

In his narrow pocket of darkness, Eli clenched his eyes shut and pinched his lips tight.

*Driver says there's trouble on the line.*

He knew the Shape in front of him was still there, waiting. Eli wanted desperately to go back to the Island of Sodor but he was terrified of what he might find there, the other engines dying, his familiar old friends turned sick and strange in the toxic light of their unwelcome new visitor. Instead he cowered, weeping silently until he was pretty sure the Shape had withdrawn and moved on.

"Safe now," he whispered. "Just like Thomas said. Safe now. Safe—"

That was when the rough hands shot forth from the blackness and yanked him out.

## 25

Mike wasn't happy to be back in the ER waiting room. He cast a grim look at the planks and boards that had been nailed over the windows. No light seeped through now, not even the nebulous late-evening variety that had existed just an hour earlier. Outside it was fully dark, must have been for a while. He remembered the keys and cell phone he'd left in the MRI suite and was about to suggest going back for them when the police officer—who had introduced himself as Hank—spoke up.

"There's a stretcher out in the hallway." Hank pointed a thick finger at Mike. Ten minutes in the company of another human being had put him firmly back in cop mode. "Take your flashlight and bring it back here."

"What are we doing?"

"Making a battering ram."

A battering ram, why hadn't he thought of that? Mike brought the stretcher back. Hank's plan was simple. They bent down and hoisted one of the sofas from the middle of the waiting room, setting it on top of the stretcher and strapping it down with canvas restraints.

"Here's the idea," Hank said. "You're gonna get behind this thing and push. I'm gonna be up front and steer. We'll get this fat-ass bitch going as fast as we can and send her right through there—" He pointed his flashlight at a big sheet of plywood covering the window to his immediate right. "You got it?"

Mike nodded. Grunting, he and the cop rolled the stretcher to the far side of the waiting room, clearing thirty feet of distance between the stretcher's launch point and the point of impact.

"What about our flashlights?" Mike asked. "We need to see where we're going with this thing."

"Prop 'em up over there." Hank nodded at a wooden shelf thirty feet away, where the waiting room's TV had once sat. "Just aim 'em toward the window."

Looking back on this moment, Mike realized he'd entered into the endeavor with the worst kind of foreboding. It wasn't until afterward that he understood this feeling for what it was: dread so dense that it bordered on a premonition. He and the cop took their places on either end of the stretcher and started pushing it, walking first and building up to a run. Within a dozen paces they'd gathered more speed than Mike had thought possible, the wheels clacking and whacking away.

As they careened through the flashlight beams, Mike caught sight of a skinny, familiar silhouette standing off to the right of the stretcher's path.

*Calhoun? Was it—*

It had to be, the security guard halfway down the hall leading to the private ER rooms, and now Mike saw he was waving at them, pointing, saying something he couldn't quite hear over the racket of the wheels and his own breathing. It sounded like—

*It sounded like he was telling them to run.*

Mike was never exactly sure what happened to Hank. He was only aware of a swift black blur flying into the front end of the stretcher from the direction Calhoun was pointing, slamming it sideways and knocking it over so the sofa hit the floor with a crash. Following it was a shriek, high and womanly, that never quite seemed to end, instead merely withering down to a wet rattle.

Pivoting, he looked back at Calhoun. The security guard was still there—riveted to the spot, staring at the place where the stretcher and the sofa had fallen, his hands clasping either side of his face. Mike had never seen an expression quite like it before, a combination of revulsion and profound dismay merged with the look of someone who had just stuck a fork into an electrical outlet. As Mike watched, Calhoun turned and burst into a rambling scarecrow run.

The last thing Mike heard before he also turned and ran into the darkness was a hard spiky spray of laughter.

## 26

**Blind without the little toy train**—she had searched everywhere for it and come up with nothing—Sarah crept into the basement corridor, feeling her way along the wall. The hospital breathed in and out around her, a cavernous black lung brought to life by the deepest sensory deprivation.

*Trust your ears, Sarah.* That was Mr. Clayton, her old piano teacher. *They'll tell you what's right before your mind does.*

Her ears, yes, but wasn't there anything more powerful in her arsenal? She'd read somewhere about the psychic bond between mothers and children, the paranormal sensitivity that comes to life when their offspring are in mortal peril. Where was that instinct now? If she could conjure up an image of these empty halls breathing around her, why couldn't she summon a vision of her son's whereabouts?

Instead she felt a thick yellow gaze pressing on her beneath layers of eddying black, unseen fingers extending toward her throat. The darkness seemed to swirl and churn. What was Snow, anyway, if he could have done what he did to the corpse on the stairwell earlier? Could she even call something like that human?

The implications of his presence had already turned Sarah's body against her. Her breathing had become irregular, a series of gasps and breaths held overlong, her heart stammering incoherently. In the darkness shapes were beginning to coalesce, leaning figures with gangling limbs, the misshapen heads stamped with oblong faces and deep, insane eyes.

*Stop. You have to stop.*

But she couldn't. Modern technology might have banished superstition, but apparently it hadn't exterminated it. How long did you need to suspend a person in total darkness before all those old fears came back? What if the occult had always been the true way of things, and science and reason simple self-delusion, a fringe benefit of artificial light?

Her fingertips grazed the wall, groping and fumbling their way over its unfamiliar texture. The tiny cracks in the concrete felt like wrinkles on a dead woman's breasts. Yet she stumbled forward, inches at a time. What was she hoping for—that she would just run into Eli down here somewhere? In the dark these hallways ran forever, intersecting and crisscrossing in defiance of all reckoning. In the depths of her reptilian brain Sarah could almost feel them lengthening in front of her, canting and tilting at sickening, German Expressionist angles, their dark recesses expanding to fill the vacuum of deepest space.

Her foot came down on something soft and she gasped, recoiling. The smell wafted up to flood her nose, raw meat, spoiled blood, triggering reflexive intimations of public restrooms, tampon dispensers, girlhood pain.

"Oh no." Did she breathe these words, or just think them? "Please, no."

Squatting, she descended on a knotted rope of heartbeats until she was kneeling, forcing herself to brush her fingers across the shape on the floor. It was soft, pliant but firm underneath, plastered with a layer of damp fabric. Her hands passed over the claylike stickiness of cold flesh, the furze of wiry hair, and the unexpected protrusion of bone, until she got a sense of the size of the thing.

Relief gushed through her. Not Eli. A man's body, one of the cops maybe, but not her son.

"Please," she whispered. "Let him be here. Let him be safe."

*Talking, Sarah? To whom, the ghosts? The dearly departed? Frank Snow? You'd have better luck beseeching the dead themselves for mercy, wouldn't you?*

Rising up, she took a broad step to the right and tripped over the second body, landing squarely on top of it. The corpse's nose pushed against her cheek, stubble scraping her chin, half-open lips brushing her mouth as she gave a strangled scream, fending off its mannequin-armed embrace. Faintly, under the blood smell, she caught a whiff of Old Spice, onions, stale urine. Stiff fingers poked at the small of her back, scratching under her shirt, probing the knobs of her lower spine.

"No!" She wrenched sideways and fought to disentangle herself. There were at least two other corpses and she was lodged between them, kicking and swinging her arms as one of the bodies released a drawn-out gargling sound from deep inside its abdomen. She spun, levered herself upright. Her hand grazed one of their thighs, encountering a long, hard shape and jolting back as if scalded.

With a scream she was up, backing away, knowing she'd betrayed her location if Snow was down here.

Gasping she leaned against the wall, literally panting with fright and panic. The moment replayed in her brain, the bodies and the singular coldness of them . . .

*Can't see! If only I could see!*

She thought of the object she'd encountered at one of the corpse's thighs, a stiff, tubular shaft.

*No,* she told herself, *I'm not reaching down there again. You don't understand. I can't.*

The seconds spun out as her heart continued thudding in her chest. She took a breath of blackness and put her hand out into its impenetrable depths. Down to where the dead men were, down the blood-encrusted length of his uniformed leg and up the seam of his trousers.

The ribbed steel case of the flashlight was exactly where she'd felt it. She tugged it free, her thumb finding the button, snapping it on.

She shined her flashlight at the bodies on the floor, her three gore-streaked Lotharios sprawled next to a linen cart that had fallen on its side. A bloody trail led around the corner. Had one of them gotten up and wandered away?

Where was Snow? Just around that corner?

*If he was down here, you'd already be lying there next to them with your throat ripped out.*

*Yes,* she thought. For the moment at least, Snow was elsewhere on other business in a different part of the hospital. The thought gave her no solace, but the flashlight did. She pointed it up the corridor, in the direction she'd come, pushing back whatever had been grasping for her out of the primordial caves just moments before.

"Eli?" she called out. "Eli, it's Mommy. Can you hear me?"

The only sound that came back was the echo of her voice. Sarah kept the flashlight beam aimed straight ahead. With the focused deliberation of a tightrope walker she placed one foot in front of the other and began her way down the long hall, calling her son's name.

## 27

**And, elsewhere: Dr. Edward Walker.**

Still alive, yes; an inmate of this same darkness, though not exactly. Here was a man who had never in his professional life entered into a situation whose outcome he felt he could not in some way influence. He stood now pressed flat against a wall, silver nitrate eyes a beacon in the black—if not of hope, then certainly of clarity. For surely, amid such confusion, any man able to rein in his fear must in his way evanesce, even shine, despite the darkness shivering around him.

He was somewhere in the labyrinthine bowels of the ground floor, sliding along the wall, senses extended for any variation in the cinder-block surface ahead of him. Moving? Yes, with great care. He had a penlight in his pocket but wouldn't yet permit himself to use it. His hands were already full. In his left, a police radio, scavenged from the corpse of the officer upstairs. And in his right hand . . .

Well, he was already considering what he needed to do with the object in his right hand.

He advanced with the patience of a man who had trusted his sense of touch for a living, palpating the darkness as he might a patient, acutely aware of any variation in temperature or texture. He knew how to move forward under adverse circumstances—moving forward, after all, was what he had been trained to do, long before medicine had become his fate—but so much was at risk. Not just his own life, but the institution whose walls he'd come to think of as an extension of himself.

*First we attack the sickness, then we protect the patient:* his own personal twist on the Hippocratic oath. Nothing he would ever admit aloud, but his religion nonetheless. Medicine was his sacred war, a red church of bone and blood. *Remember the awe you felt the first day of Gross Anatomy, scalpel in hand; hold on to that awe, take a little every day, it will immunize you against fear.* In the end fear, not death, was the killer.

Walker was not a young man anymore, or even middle aged; no, now he was old, and death knew his location at all times. He and death were old acquaintances, more intimate than his wife, his mistresses, or his colleagues. Trauma, cancer, infection—the particulars were endless. Despite Walker's best efforts to protect and preserve life, so many children had clutched his hand at the end, so many slipped away. Tonight Walker sensed them gazing back at him from out of the dark, so real that if he turned on his penlight he would see them gathered silently around him, a pale topiary of upraised faces.

He put the police radio in his lab coat pocket, took out his penlight and shone it on the wall, spilling shadows with an irregular recklessness that bothered him. Yet there was something invigorating about it, too. His hearing was not especially keen anymore, his night vision poor, but his sense of touch had saved hundreds of lives, and he felt a hot, almost erotic thrill to be using it now to save his own. Surely such adrenaline was the sole province of those who could count the remainder of their lives in hours or less. There was power in the inevitability of it. As he slipped his hands deeper into the enormous skull of this place, Walker knew that in some way his entire career had been leading up to his own appointment with death.

*Even you are not immune, old friend,* the dry voice whispered. *Not to me.*

*I know,* Walker thought. In the end he carried only one coin to pay with, the only one that meant anything. The spirit in which he'd seen people give in to death were legion—anger, bravery, defiance, tears, relief, and none of it mattered any more than the shroud in which they wound the corpse.

Tonight, though, Walker meant to do everything in his power before he paid up. When he gave up his life he meant to get the best possible price. Given the circumstances, it was the least he could do.

He turned his head to the object in his right hand. It was a book, very old, eccentrically shaped and heavier than one might have expected. As Walker moved forward, it rode against his hip, its binding rustling with his gait, making the dry pages crackle with a noise like that of October leaves.

"The good doctor," a voice behind him said, "alone in the dark, sir?"

Walker didn't have a chance to turn before an open hand slammed his head into the wall. The penlight fell to the floor. Walker felt his world torque crookedly on its axis and reached out for balance, cursing his own sloppiness, but it was too late. Eager hands were fastening on the book, prying it loose from his fingers.

"Frank," Dr. Walker said. "No!"

"Don't worry," Snow's voice said, somewhere in the darkness, "I'll take good care of it, as if it were my own. You of all people should know that."

"You don't know—"

"What?" Fingers pinned his throat to the wall like an iron collar. "What don't I know?"

Walker tried to answer but his voice box couldn't squeeze out the words. He was getting close to losing consciousness when the hand released him and let him drop on his knees to the floor.

"I'll see you again soon," Snow's voice said. "Watch for me when I bring the light."

## 28

Calhoun had never intended to hide out in the chapel. He'd simply bolted from the emergency room, an orphan of blind velocity and questionable instinct, the collusion of which had brought him here.

He remembered the chain of events leading up to his escape clearly enough, up to a point. One second he had been barricaded in the ER room and heard voices, Mike's and somebody else. Sticking his head out into the hall, Calhoun saw the waiting room illuminated by crisscrossed flashlight beams, the racket of wheels filling open space as a stretcher flashed by with a couch strapped to it. That was when he saw the shadow that made him shout at them to run. The next second the shadow wasn't even touching the floor, it was flying from the far side of the room like a hawk on a field mouse and the cop—

Well, the cop was just gone.

Calhoun stopped processing at that point, making no further attempt to put the events in order and make sense of them. Motion took over. It had been less like running, more as if the floor of the world had gone vertical, flinging him through the ER exit, where utter blackness engulfed him like a man falling off an ocean liner at midnight. The screams and gargles and laughter ripping through the darkness behind him, the frantic slap and sting of running feet headed in the opposite direction—none of these distractions registered. Calhoun just kept going straight ahead, an arrow fired from the bowstring of his own neural plexus. And still it felt like he was traveling down.

He couldn't see—with his eyes, anyway. But after the initial disorientation had whisked away, he realized how much he remembered. He was stone cold sober now, a rarity for this time of night, and he was surprised at how clearly his memory conjured up the main-floor concourse that he'd walked down tens of thousands of times.

Up ahead he could sense the concourse broadening around him. Yes . . . That would be the main information desk coming up on his right, the hospital admissions to the left, a warren of administration offices nobody had used for ages. Past the row of architecturally useless Doric pillars that signaled the end of the lobby, the hallway would become a thinner tributary, and if Calhoun just kept going straight ahead—

*Whack!* A great clanking chandelier of pain swung through his center of gravity as he collided with the last of the pillars, bright pinwheels corkscrewing through his inner ears, and for an instant he stepped back dazed on his heels.

From somewhere behind him the glow of a more real light was coming up the concourse toward him.

*It's him.*

Stumbling away, shaking off the fireworks, Calhoun started running again. He could sense Snow's light getting closer, gaining ground behind him, and he knew without a doubt that he was running into a blind alley, the remaining exits severely restricted. Soon his choices would be limited to a flight of stairs leading to the upper floors of the North Wing, or—

Without another thought his hands found the door to his left and grabbed it, levering his body inside and whooshing the door shut behind him.

*Let him think I went upstairs.*

He crouched, listening, listening.

*Let him think, oh let him think . . .*

As time drew its long blade, Calhoun came unclenched, realizing only now where his feet had chosen to deposit him. He had literally found sanctuary in the hospital's nondenominational chapel, the oldest part of the original building, erected back at the end of the nineteenth century from the original stones the workmen dug out of the field when they'd first broken ground.

It was pitch-black in here, too: Calhoun couldn't see any better than he'd been able to out there. His sense of smell grew sharper, and he caught a whiff of old prayer candles, greasy tapers whose tallow had long ago guttered to puddles. Calhoun recognized the odor. After his father left, his mother had dragged him to church, planted his small bottom in a wooden pew, making him sit through endless hallelujahs and visions of kingdom come. Now, hunkered in the dark, he had an odd thought: unlike most chapels, few souls had ever come here to praise God or to thank Him. They knelt in extreme desperation, to plead mercy for themselves or their loved ones, to gain understanding or discharge toxic levels of grief. Maybe they had been granted a reprieve; probably not. This had never been a place of joy or worship but a septic landfill for panic and pain.

*Skritch-skrii-iitch . . .*

He twisted in the direction of the door so hard he heard his neck crack. He was almost sure he'd imagined it, but as he waited, pacing off the intervening seconds as a man in jail might pace the dimensions of his cell, the scratching noise came again.

*Skriitchh.*

It persisted, just outside the door. Like a dirty fingernail dragging across the inner lining of a grave.

*Skrrii-iii-iii . . .*

A skein of coldness wound around his flesh and drew tight. He thought about Snow, his mind producing a very clear picture of the man leaning against the other side of the door, patiently tapping and scratching the wood.

*But that doesn't make any sense. Why would he . . . ?*

His mind pulsed back to what he'd seen up on the sixth floor, after Dr. Walker had spoken those words. What he'd seen there defied all logic. Yet it had burrowed so deeply into his brain that he could no longer deny that it happened.

*Skkkrrriiiii—*

Calhoun's breath froze at his lips.

The sound was *inside* the chapel with him.

*Impossible, but—*

It was drawing nearer.

Perhaps, he thought, it had been in here with him the whole time, slinking ever closer in the dark, seeking him out, enjoying the fear rolling off him in waves. Calhoun still hadn't drawn a breath.

*If I hold perfectly still . . . if I don't breathe . . .*

As he listened, it became louder and more distinct until he felt as though it was directly in front of him.

*What if it's in your head?*

In the silence the awful blind man's landscape ballooned around him, stretching at the seams. Calhoun took a step in the direction he thought the door might be and discovered that he'd not only lost all sense of orientation, he'd also lost the strength to move.

He thought of the enormous crucifix that hung at the front of the chapel, seized by the irrational certainty that the cross was hanging upside down in the darkness. He smelled sweat and rotten blood. The same suspicion insisted that the body nailed to its planks would not be Christ. No, it would be the most recent victim of the thing making the scratching sound, and very soon Calhoun would be joining it. He felt his sinuses pop as if the barometric pressure inside the room had plunged.

*Your father went crazy at the end, too, Stevie.*

Dry-ice vapor crowded his lungs.

*They found him behind that boardinghouse, trying to stand up. The can of paint he'd been drinking was still in his hand. He said he heard noises, he was trying to run away—*

*Daddy wasn't crazy!*

*The sins of the father shall be visited on the son.*

*No, Mama! I'm not crazy! I'm not—*

As if to discourage the thought, the scratching noise came back around behind him, more eagerly now.

Without another thought, Calhoun broke ranks and ran forward, hands wavering crazily in front of him. He found a wall and swept its surface until his fingers located the edge of a door with the bolt he'd slammed home when he'd first come in. He yanked it open and flew out, gasping in the slightly warmer, fresher air of the outer corridor, still racing, pounding his way forward until he reached the stairwell to the North Wing. He hit the door running and flew as fast as he could up the steps.

Footsteps slammed the stairs behind him. The thing was at his heels, coming up fast.

*All those empty bottles in the trash every week, and the trashmen stood and laughed—*

Calhoun gripped the banister to his right and followed it up to the next stairwell, his legs already feeling limp beneath him. His lungs clotted. Nothing in his body worked right. His stamina, never the most reliable of phenomena, was staging a mutiny, abandoning ship.

*He said he was trying to run away.*

He somehow found the strength to keep running.

**29.**

Jolie's camera, the one she'd brought in to snap pictures of the hospital, was a silver Olympus Stylus—hardly the most expensive model on the market. She'd bought it a year ago to take on a cruise and barely removed it from its box, but the cute Best Buy salesman had done his job. It had all the basic bells and whistles, autofocus, turbo-zoom, along with a bunch of features she probably hadn't even discovered.

Tonight the only thing that mattered to her was the battery and the built-in flash. It had gotten her this far, to her current location on the fourth floor of the South Wing.

Intent on discovering the source of the explosion earlier, she had only just stumbled onto the sixth floor when the power had gone out. At that point common sense had won a brief scrimmage with curiosity, and Jolie had slowly made her way back down the stairs only to discover that the way out was locked.

Now, repeating the ritual that had allowed her slow progress through the darkness, she raised the camera's streamlined shape in front of her face and pressed the button, triggering the flash. A silent, two-beat electrical storm battered the hallway in front of her, engraving its layout on her retinas before the blackness swept back over it.

After her pupils readjusted, she looked down at the camera's small glowing screen, studying the photo that she'd just snapped. It showed a long straight corridor with a row of doors on either side. To her right was a stretcher, a fire extinguisher, and, farther down, a bag of laundry, her outermost landmark. The number of the nearest door was 4117.

She was getting close.

Her motivation for heading to the psych ward, up on the fourth floor, was so simple it was almost laughable. It had an open-air exercise court. Jolie thought if she could get up there, she'd at least be able to get out, even if it was only into starlight. Her head would clear. And she could climb—

*Don't think about that yet. Just see what you find.*

Staring at a digital image on the back of the camera, she brought her foot forward again, tapping the edge of her toe against the bag of laundry that appeared in the left lower corner of the screen. It was odd navigating the hall by a still photo; she almost expected to see herself step into the picture.

She stopped and snapped again, flooding the hall with another pulse of light.

In the new image, the hallway looked shorter. A sepia-encrusted canvas straitjacket lay right in the middle of the floor. Up ahead she could see the doorway off to the right, forty feet away, that led to the outdoor exercise area. It had been built on top of one of the hospital's many low-level additions, three stories up, a full-sized basketball court for the psych patients, completely enclosed in twenty-foot-high chain link. Jolie had been up here only once before, to pick up a paranoid schizophrenic for a brain MRI, but she remembered the basketball court, and if her memory served, the only part that wasn't enclosed was the top. If she could climb up there and then lower herself back down the other side, she'd be on top of the roof, pretty high up, it was true, but maybe . . .

She'd cross that bridge when she got to it. First, though, she had to get outside.

Arms extended, she advanced into the dark hallway, made herself take ten steps, raised the camera for another picture, put her finger on the shutter . . . and stopped.

Someone was coming up the stairs in front of her.

Coming fast, too, either chasing something or being chased. Either way, she was in the wrong place at the wrong time. As soon as he got to the landing, whoever it was would be blasting right through that door.

Ahead of her in the darkness, the running footsteps gained volume and intensity, superimposed over her pounding heart.

Jolie jerked the camera up and hit the button for one last picture. Another double-pulse of light winked at the walls, momentarily blinding her, and she waited in agony while her eyes adjusted enough to see the photo on the camera's screen.

The image showed the shortened hallway as before. But now the door at the end was swinging open, a blur of something coming toward her, frozen in a shutter too slow to catch its shape.

All she could see was its eyes, wild and sick, caught in the camera's flash.

Then, while she was still looking at its image on the screen, the shape rammed past her in the dark, knocking her sideways against the wall, and she almost dropped the camera. A whiff of hair tonic, cigarettes, and cheap cologne passed through her nose and she thought of Calhoun. He was already blundering past her, farther down the dark hall, the way that she'd come, tripping and crashing into obstacles that she'd passed over by taking pictures of them along the way.

She almost called his name but stopped.

The thing that had been chasing him up the stairs was still coming toward her, no subtlety in its eagerness. She could feel it hammering forward at incredible speed, feet scraping the floor, pushing a wall of foul-smelling air in front of it. In the darkness it felt about as human as a runaway train.

Groping for the camera, Jolie flipped it over to hide the bluish glow of its screen and plastered her back and shoulders as tightly as possible to the wall as the thing careened past, powerfully enough to riffle her hair. There was a great, complicated clattering sound down at the far end of the hall, a door slammed, then silence.

She tensed for the sound of Calhoun's screams.

But there were no screams.

There was nothing at all.

# 30.

Calhoun had seen the light at the end of the hallway just moments after he'd exploded through the stairwell door onto the fourth floor. He thought it could've been a hallucination, a mere side effect of his own panic . . . at least until the moment he'd opened that last door.

The secondary glow wasn't like that initial flash of light as he'd sprinted out of the stairwell. He hadn't imagined that—the flash of a camera—and through his dark-adapted eyes he could've sworn he'd even glimpsed a figure standing behind it, actually holding a camera. And even in his semihysterical state, that was irrefutably crazy. Who in the unholy name of fuck would be up here in the dark in an abandoned hospital taking pictures?

He'd run toward the light as fast as he could, his chest cramped and burning too badly to give whoever it was fair warning that Snow was behind him with all the hounds of hell on his trail. Given world enough and time, Calhoun would have liked to have shouted some warning, however incoherent, but his foot had tangled on something in his path and he would've gone sailing had he not caught his grip on the railing that ran at waist-level along the wall of the corridor.

*This is it,* he thought grimly. *This is where he takes me, if he's going to. He won't get a better opportunity than this.*

But nothing touched him.

Calhoun exhaled slowly, breath draining from his mouth and nose. The fevered footsteps of a moment earlier had stopped. If Snow was behind him somewhere, he was moving on tiptoe again. Which, when Calhoun thought about it, made about as much sense as the mystery paparazzo somewhere up the hallway snapping photographs.

Suddenly his attention was arrested by something else, something in front of him in the blackness. Significantly in front of him, actually. Calhoun blinked, not trusting his eyes, and looked more closely at it, straining to spot the magician's trick.

Down at the far end of the hall was a thin line of light escaping from under a distant door. It was plain and perfectly straight, as if some steady hand had taken a scalpel and made an incision into the belly of the darkness itself.

He couldn't be sure, but he would've sworn it hadn't been there a moment earlier.

*How would you know? A moment earlier you were running for your life!*

True . . . but even in a state of extreme sphincter-constriction, wouldn't he have noticed a light in front of him shining underneath a door in an otherwise pitch-black hallway? Could he have actually missed it?

*Maybe, maybe not.*

One thing was certain. Snow wasn't down there. Snow was still somewhere behind him, and Calhoun, who had been scrambling for his life a moment earlier, knew there was no way he could've gotten in front of him. And why would he, without attacking Calhoun on the way?

Conclusion: there was someone else in the room at the far end of the hall.

His feet started making their way in a series of slow, cautious half-measures, like two blind rats creeping through a maze of traps and poison. With every step he anticipated Snow's cold hands seizing his throat from behind, the jag of the blade ripping into the flesh of his back, lifting him up off his feet. Of course, he couldn't really anticipate such unimaginable pain without experiencing it. If it happened, Calhoun just hoped it would be quick.

Was Snow watching him in the dark, playing with him? Had he actually lost track of him somewhere between the stairs and the hall?

Impossible.

*Then why aren't I dead?*

He stared harder at the light under the door.

A peculiar thought shot to the forefront of his mind, irrational as hell, but if life had taught him anything it was that the mind always had time for the irrational. The irrational was A-list. No matter how busy things were, it always got a seat.

What if whatever was behind that door was so bad that even Frank Snow himself had turned around rather than go toward it?

Calhoun grunted at the sheer preposterousness of the idea. Of course, what was behind the door at the end of the hallway was just a light. Maybe a cop with a flashlight, maybe just a flashlight with no cop, maybe his own mind blowing fuses on him, or—

Maybe it was the other thing.

He thought again about what he'd seen when he was with Dr. Walker and Snow in that dusty, toy-filled room on the sixth floor. He remembered Walker's creepy incantation, if that's what you could call it, and how he, Calhoun, had even at that moment thought to himself, *Is this guy actually saying this?* And, of course, the answer had been yes, because nobody else was speaking. He remembered the thing that had happened when the door was closed, and what it had looked like down there, before Calhoun had the presence of mind to look away. He remembered how it had made him want to scream, to pluck his eyes out, leaving only sightless holes, which, ironically enough, would have given him almost exactly what he'd seen up until now.

He looked again at the light under the door.

What if he opened this door and saw it again? Would he scream then? *Oh, yes.* Would he tear out his eyes? All hyperbole aside, Calhoun thought there was a very good chance he would.

Yet here he stood before it just the same, in a kind of nerve-brutalized wonderment, watching his own hand reaching for the knob.

He turned it and opened the door, and stared inside.

The dead woman dangling inside had a huge red grin smeared over her face.

Calhoun stared at her, her name already popping into his head: Mona Homely.

He'd heard about her years ago from the security guard who had actually discovered her body. She was a nurse who had hanged herself here in the hospital for reasons unknown. Calhoun saw her now, as he heard she'd been then, naked and purple, her young body fast-forwarded into sudden old age by the exigencies of strangulation. Blood and gravity had sausaged her legs and feet, fattening them into white-stocking loaves that dangled eighteen inches above her neatly folded nurse's uniform on the floor. Her head hung at a slight angle, just so, as if in mock-consternation or disapproval. The blank eyes and smeared red lipstick stared back at Calhoun from the coifed helmet of blond hair, and he saw her mouth twitch. *That's because of the bugs in there,* he thought dumbly. *The bugs are already eating her insides out.*

He scrunched his eyes shut and made himself breathe, his heart going like a jazz drummer cranked out of his mind on crystal meth. It was stress, nothing more. Everything he'd seen up until now, all he'd been through, was finally backing up so grossly that he was, was—

*Crazy like your father, stumble-bum syphilitic raving out of his mind—*

There was no suicidal ICU nurse in the supply closet; in fact, maybe what he'd seen up on the sixth floor had been a similar apparition. Maybe . . .

He opened his eyes in time to see her painted lips curling up, only slightly, as what first looked like a tiny black hair pushed itself out of the folds of her mouth. Calhoun's vision sharpened. The gleaming roachlike insect at least the size of a quarter squirmed free and began crawling up Mona Homely's cheek, toward her open eye, where it dangled momentarily from her lower lash like a single black tear before scuttling over the glossy white surface of the sclera.

Calhoun flung the door shut with a bang and stood back in the darkness, staring at it. He looked at the light that still bled out from underneath. Real or imagined, the vision of Mona Homely's corpse still hung in his mind's eye. Calhoun realized that he'd seen something else that the man who'd first found her had not reported.

She'd been wearing a silver crucifix.

It had been dangling upside down.

## 31

Jolie was out.

In the most recent photo she'd taken, the door leading to the psychiatric ward's outdoor basketball court appeared as a simple metal-reinforced glass sheet with a chrome handle. If it was locked, she was prepared to pitch the fire extinguisher through it, but that proved unnecessary. The handle turned with nothing more than a rusty squeak and, praise Allah, she boogied right through. *Simplest thing in the world, ladies and germs, even the hospital floozy could do it.*

She took in a deep breath and blew the hair from her eyes. Despite the fact that it was completely enclosed in high chain-link fencing, the court immediately made her feel like she'd escaped. The night breeze bristling against her bare forearms and neck smelled of freshly mowed grass and the fishy stink of fertilizer from farms far away.

*I never thought shit could smell so good,* she thought, a trembling little smile twitching halfway over her face.

She looked up. Somewhere up in the vicinity of weather satellites, a dense heap of clouds sopped up the hazy moonlight, and when the clouds began to drift westward the hooked lunar crescent spilled down brightly enough that Jolie didn't need the camera's flash to make her way forward.

If she could climb up the fence and lower herself down the other side, then she would really be out. There had to be a fire escape or some kind of maintenance ladder going down the outside of the hospital. Twenty minutes from now she'd be in her car, driving away from here as fast as humanly possible. She'd be sure to alert the police that there were others inside, but first she was going to get the hell out of here. *Sorry, sports fans, but it's every woman for herself.*

She reached the fence, shoved the camera in her purse, looped the strap over her shoulder, and started up.

Climbing was harder than it looked. The spaces where the wires crisscrossed were slightly smaller than the tips of her shoes, making it more difficult to catch a foothold. Cold wires pinched her fingers, and the fence was built on an inward slope, all of which was no doubt deliberate to keep the monkeys inside the monkey house. She listened to the soft jingling and ringing of fence wires and metal posts as she pulled herself up, hand over hand, and didn't look back.

Far above, a new pile of clouds floated back over the moon, sucking up the light.

Below her, she heard the door squeak open.

Clinging to the fence, Jolie peered down into the darkness of the basketball court, her eyes flicking frantically for a trace of movement in the imperfect light. Without losing her grip she managed to reach down and take the camera from her purse, aiming it and hitting the button.

There was a flash, and in its brief pulse she glimpsed a figure in orange halfway across the court, smeared by motion.

Jolie pressed the button again. The flash burst, illuminating the exercise court below.

The orange-clad figure was gone.

She looked down at the camera.

His face covered the screen, as if zoomed in close. Its lopsided grin filled the blue rectangle, the corner of its mouth and one crazed eye.

Something grabbed her ankle.

Screaming, yanking her leg free, she dropped the camera and clawed at the fence, wrenching her body upward in spastic jerks and jolts. Now she didn't even feel the wire as it bit into the tender webbing between her fingers. The only thing that existed was the fence; the only thing that mattered was getting over it.

Below her, the flash pulsed over and over, taking pictures of her.

Jolie climbed faster. Bright sacs of heretofore unfelt chemicals ruptured through her bloodstream, and without realizing it she was moving effortlessly, chugging past pain and exhaustion, every muscle synchronized, able to climb forever if she had to. Her body felt weightless, rising up on its own momentum.

Far below her now, the camera's flash blazed again and again, convulsively. She could hear him down there chuckling.

Jolie jerked her head up toward the top of the fence, amazed to see how close she was. Within seconds she would be at the top, swinging her leg over, lowering herself down the other side.

She didn't notice that the camera had stopped flashing, or the faint jingling sounds of chain link against steel poles as Snow climbed along behind her. She just looked through the fence and thought how she would get down. It was twenty feet, maybe more; for an instant she considered jumping, but if she twisted her ankle on the other side and couldn't run, then—

Something brushed the top of her head and she looked up, startled at the feeling of ropes against her face from above.

*Oh God. No. NO—*

The basketball court was covered, after all.

Not by metal bars or fence, but a mesh of thin black netting that went from one side to the other. Its shadow in the moonlight lay across Jolie's cheek like a widow's veil. She hadn't been able to see it from down below, the netting being so dark and so fine, but of course it was there, it would have to be there, to keep the would-be suicides from climbing over.

Snow's hand found her calf and squeezed.

Jolie screamed again, the toes of her work sneakers squeaking off, losing their hold, leaving her dangling momentarily by one hand. Catching her grip, she felt a long ice cube drip of sweat between her shoulder blades as she struggled to pull away.

Then he was on her, pinning her body tight to the fence with his own. She could smell and feel the powerful flow of his breath over her shoulder, flooding her nose with every imaginable odor of decay.

"Please." Through her fright she hardly heard what he was saying. "God, please . . . please, you don't have to do this. Please, let me—"

Through the prism of tears she saw him release his grip on the chain link on the right side of her head, leaning back so the only thing keeping him upright was his left hand.

*Oh, thank you.*

His free hand went down and drew out the object dangling from a loop on his jumpsuit.

It was some type of sharpened metal rod, the oversized bit of a surgical drill, some orthopedic tool he must have scavenged from the operating room. It looked well over a foot long, an object designed for gouging large holes in cartilage and bone. *He's going to use that on me,* her mind gibbered, *this can't be happening, you're having a nightmare, Jolie, this doesn't happen to girls from central Pennsylvania, wake up, for the love of God, wake up, WAKE UP—*

Her eyes widened. Even screaming, the nightmare was still there.

*"Stop! I can help you!"*

The drill hung motionless below her, Snow's face materializing next to it. "Pretty pie," he said. "Mommy's little love, Daddy's little hope, twice as sweet as honey, twice as clean as soap."

"Please."

"What makes you think I need your help, pretty pie?"

"You . . . you made a map."

"Map?"

"Of the hospital," Jolie said, "on a Bible page, showing all the exits. So you could find your way out. The cops took it from you. I can help you get out."

Now he was almost laughing. "What makes you think I want out?"

She stared at him.

"Oh, you can help me, all right, pretty pie." He raised the drill bit up to her face. "You can put this in your mouth."

"What?"

"Suck on it. You remember how to do that, don't you?"

Before she quite knew it, Jolie found herself complying. She opened her mouth to respond and almost instantly felt curved metal press eagerly over her lips, clicking against her teeth, the hooked end of the drill bit grazing her tongue, triggering her gag reflex. She shut her eyes. It didn't help. Not at all.

"Careful now. Don't hurt yourself."

She slipped a little and felt the drill bit twisting just barely, unexpectedly, nicking the inner velvet of her cheek. Salty blood trickled over her molars and down her throat. The drill withdrew.

Snow didn't talk. Maybe it was the light, but his face appeared thinner, gaunter, some critical moment of slippage taking place. For the first time since the lights went out she was reminded of how sick Snow had looked when she had first laid eyes on him. He looked like that again, now, coming down off a manic cycle.

"Now get on down from there." He raised the drill, blunt-end first. "Time to put the rest of the night into motion."

"I don't—"

She saw the blunt end coming at her, so close that she saw two of them, one on either side, then blackness.

## 32

*Eli?*

In his hiding place in the basement storage room, he opened his eyes, almost involuntarily. He hadn't been sleeping exactly, though he sensed an indistinct slab of time had slipped past without his knowing it, like when he woke up in the middle of the night and heard his parents snoring in the other room. His body felt cold and cramped except for where he'd been clutching himself, his palms and armpits, where the fabric of his shirt was moist with perspiration and, as he rearranged his limbs, swiftly became cold upon exposure to the air.

Then he remembered the hands.

They'd pulled his shirt up in the darkness and he'd felt something slashing over his skin, making big up-and-down and sideways lines all over his chest and shoulders and back. It hadn't hurt exactly, but it was wet. There was an inky smell, too, and a squeaking noise that reminded him of Magic Markers on a dry-erase board he had at home, the one where his mommy wrote down errands. Some uncertain time later, the hands yanked his shirt down and shoved him back into the closet again.

Thinking back on it, fresh tears welled in his eyes, making the dried ones crackle up against his eyelashes.

*Hullo, there. Hi! It's me. Don't cry.*

He caught his breath, bit his lip, and listened. It was the voice of Thomas again, but fainter now, coming from somewhere far away.

*Listen. You have to listen to me.*

He couldn't answer.

*Just listen, Eli, okay?*

He nodded, his face tightened into an eye-clenched mask, and listened.

At first there was nothing. Not even the distant little creaks and dripping noises he'd heard every few minutes as he'd curled back here, phasing in and out of awareness.

But then, in the very remote periphery, he heard a sound—a thin and far-off voice—coming from outside the closet door, down one of the dark halls.

He raised his head, opening his eyes.

". . . Eli . . . ?"

He recognized the voice.

". . . Eli . . . ?"

It was his mommy.

He sat up fast, fingers clutching for the door he'd pulled closed behind him, and heard the other voice pipe up vigorously from wherever it was inside his mind.

*NO!* Thomas said. *Not a word! Promise me! Promise me you won't!*

"No, it's her!" Eli said aloud. "It's her, I hear her voice! It's my—"

*No, Eli. You can't. You mustn't. Do you understand? It might be a trap! I told you, there's trouble on the line!*

But Eli would listen to no more of it. Grabbing the door handle, he twisted it hard and threw his weight forward. The door swung open easily and he spilled out into the hall, tripping over his feet and landing in a lake of light that had already sprung forward to find him there. He lifted his head and stared into the dazzling center of the light, tears running down either side of his face, unable to see what was behind him.

"M-Mommy . . . ?"

The light swung down and in an instant she was kneeling there with him, his mother, holding him tightly and kissing him, saying his name and crying. He latched on to her, felt how hard her heart was beating, and immediately began crying, too—with fear, love, and throbbing waves of newly realized relief.

"I'm sorry, Mommy. I'm sorry I got lost. I won't do it again, I promise. I love you."

"Shh," she said. "It's okay. It's okay now. Mommy's here. Oh, thank God, thank God . . ." She picked him up and squeezed him, and he almost couldn't breathe, but that was okay because it meant she was real and not just something he was seeing in his head. "Are you okay? Are you hurt?"

"No . . ." Eli's mind flashed to the hands that had reached in earlier, the ticklish feeling against his skin, but he pushed the memory away. He was all right now, his mommy was here and she was happy, and he felt bad enough about running away. No reason to bring that up, not now.

She kissed him and loosened her grip a little but didn't put him down. "You're sure?"

"I was hiding. He came to where I was but then he went away."

"Oh, thank you, God." She looked like she was going to start crying again but it was just a single tear that escaped from her eye and she just let it hang there like a tiny beautiful stone. "I'm so glad. . . . I'm just so glad. I can't tell you what I was thinking. I'm never going to lose you again."

"Mommy?"

"Yes, baby?"

"Where's Daddy?"

"Daddy?" At first the question didn't seem to make sense to her, the way things sometimes didn't if Eli wasn't saying his words clearly enough. Except he knew that she understood what he'd asked, so why did she take so long to answer?

"I don't know, honey."

"Did the Snowman get him?"

His mommy looked at him and shook her head slowly. It didn't make him feel as good as he'd hoped, and for some reason he found himself wishing she would've said the word "no" instead of shaking her head in that haunted, silent way. But she didn't say anything.

"What are we going to do?"

"We're getting out of here."

"What about . . ."

"It'll be okay," she said. "I promise."

Eli nodded. That was enough, more than enough. She rose to her feet, lifting him onto her shoulder, holding the flashlight under her arm, and the love he felt for her at that moment was transcendent.

She carried him down one hallway into another, through a doorway that

Eli realized was his daddy's work area, MRI. His head began to feel impossibly heavy. He wanted to ask where they were going next, but the steady rocking motion of her gait was like a sedative lulling him to sleep. Right now all he wanted to do was rest in her arms.

In MRI, she picked up her car keys and her cell phone. She pushed a button on the phone. *Beep.* "Damn it," she murmured.

"What's the . . ." *matter, Mommy,* was what Eli intended to ask, but in the middle of the question, he fell asleep.

# 33.

Mike's decision to return to the basement was brought on by the realization that it was the last place he'd heard his son's voice; even if it was just through the police radio, it was still the only lead he had. Unspeakable things had transpired since then, but he couldn't permit himself to think about those things. He had to go back down and look for Sarah and Eli.

He went down the stairs, shining the flashlight on the registration desk, listening to the tapping and creaking sounds of his feet on the linoleum. Going left would take him to shipping and receiving, past an entirely alternate wing of laundry and food service areas sprawling for what seemed like whole acres. To the right was MRI, CT, X-ray, where he'd been when he'd heard Eli through the walkie-talkie.

He started down the hallway again, keeping the flashlight low and wishing for the hundredth time there was a way he could use it without revealing his position. This was one of five long corridors running parallel to one another, conjoined by a honeycomb of smaller subspecialty offices, changing bays, and diagnostic suites with multiple entrances and exits. Limited to a dying flashlight, he was lucky to keep from driving his head into a wall.

He stopped, snapped the light off. There was the sound of something coming, metal dragging concrete, a rusty knife, or—

He chose his escape at random, jumping through the door and shutting it behind him. He made himself count to three hundred in the dark, extremely slowly. When he still didn't hear any sound from the hall, he turned on the flashlight again.

The file room.

It was huge, occupying what felt like a full corner of the ground floor. On every wall, towering stacks of thousands of individual patient records waited for the transportation crews that would ship them to new facilities. Shelves rose up to an industrial skyline of dead light fixtures. In the center, an abstract geometric shape formed by desks and tables contained several computers, copy machines, and phones. Mike hadn't spent much time among the desks. The bifocal-wearing bitch-goddesses who captained the hospital from behind those rectilinear slabs always seemed to be not-quite-whispering about whose whore daughter had gotten a black eye from her ex-con boyfriend, or whose baby was born with a hole in its heart because its mother had freebased while pregnant.

They'd whispered about him, too, him and Jolie.

Mike turned. The flashlight beam caught one of the printers and he saw a single sheet of paper lying on top.

It was the control sheet, the one that had been printed up when the cops had first brought Frank Snow here for his brain MRI.

Mike looked at the paper for a long time, then up at the file room stacks. Row after row of folders, thousands of lives made flat and packed away, well on their way to oblivion. Frank Snow would be one of those lives. He was in here somewhere, wasn't he? Was there something here that could help them? It was a long shot, but long shots were all he had left.

Mike checked the different-colored numbers that were adhered to the jackets until he was in Snow's neighborhood. Getting closer, he slowed down, forcing himself up on a stool that had been left here, and shined the flashlight up.

America's bogeyman was just another cardboard jacket, thicker than he'd expected, featuring rows of typed and printed bar-code labels across the front that tracked Snow's medical history at Tanglewood.

According to the front of the file, Snow had been born October 16, 1970. His most recent visit was only a year ago.

The jacket slipped and hit the floor, spilling out subfolders. The one for MRI jumped out at him. Crouching down, flashlight clamped under his arm again, he pulled Snow's films from his last visit. It was a brain scan like the one they were supposed to have done tonight. Mike held the film up to the flashlight, studying them with a technologist's eye.

The enhanced axial pictures showed a dime-sized spot in Snow's cerebellum, encircled in a ring of bright signal. The same mass showed up through all the different pictures.

*A brain tumor?*

Mike shoved the MRI aside and dug deeper into the jacket, traveling back in time. There were chest X-rays, skull X-rays, OR reports, blood tests, and a complete cardiac and neurological workup. More OR reports. Notes from Pediatric ICU attending physicians.

He glanced at the earliest of the dates: May 12, 1974.

Snow had first come to Tanglewood when he was three years old, the same age that Eli was now.

Mike flipped the page and struggled to decipher the individual's writing.

*Patient is status-post MVA, unresponsive at scene, acute neurological deficit . . .*

MVA meant motor vehicle accident. The details were written in the initial triage report, either by a nurse or the EMT on the scene, along with a diagram showing the extent of the boy's injuries. Snow's mother had been the driver, her father the passenger, neither of them wearing seat belts, both killed on impact. Snow, the only one of them properly restrained, had arrived at Tanglewood in a state of deep unconsciousness.

Mike tracked his progress with his fingertip, scanning past pages of handwritten assessments made during the weeks that three-year-old Snow had languished in his bed, eating, breathing, and voiding his waste through a complex network of valves, tubes, and stopcocks.

As he read through the handwritten pages, one style of penmanship began to dominate with great sloping paragraphs of notes. The doctor's comparatively tidy block letters became more of a hectic scrawl. At times the ballpoint had actually gouged little holes in the triplicate sheet where he'd been logging Snow's progress. Other times, whoever was writing it seemed to begin a sentence and then stop midway through, slashing out entire thoughts with a single stroke.

Mike flipped another page and looked down at a rat's nest of handwriting, nearly illegible now: *Pt. worsening, febrile with diminished BP, recommend more aggressive treatment in light of steadily deteriorating mental status. Correlate with—*

Mike flipped the page over, but there was no more.

Someone had removed it.

## 34

"Please . . ."

Calhoun heard the voice crying out on his way upstairs, just past the fifth-floor stairwell. It was little more than a stifled croak but it carried through the emptiness just the same.

"Help me."

He froze on the landing, realization soaking through him in a crimson stain, and nudged the stairwell door aside and listened again.

"For God's sake . . . someone, please . . ."

When he'd first heard the voice he had been on his way topside to gain access to the roof, having ruled out his only other option, which was the underground tunnel in the basement. There was no way he was going down into that long, dark tunnel—if Snow caught him in there he'd have no way out. The roof at least offered the comfort of starlight and relatively unobstructed terrain where he could wait out the rest of the night. And if worse came to worst, he could jump.

The voice cried: "Is anyone here?"

Calhoun cat-eyed his way down the hallway, using his peripheral vision, where he'd heard there were more rods and cones, or something. He didn't know these floors like he did the downstairs and didn't trust his radar enough to move forward, but he found himself inching along just the same, little by little, a man on a narrow ledge. His hands slithered ahead along the wall, letting his fingers do the walking, doing a Helen Keller routine for the railing.

All at once a bright light snapped on in his face, making him cringe back and throw up his hands to protect his eyes.

"Who are you?" a voice asked.

Calhoun lowered his hands, squinting, pupils shrinking. The old woman hunched in front of him had one hand fastened to her IV pole and the other locked onto an ancient silver flashlight that looked like it might've been new with Nixon. Her familiar green eyes were milky with cataracts, and her hair was a flamboyant iron wreck that stuck up and out like an old cat that couldn't decide whether it was going to jump.

Then Calhoun saw her mouth, puckered around the absence of dentures, and her face came together.

*"Ma?"*

"Stevie?" She shuffled toward him, gripping the flashlight. "Is that you?"

"I'm not seeing this."

"What's happening?" she asked. "Where is everybody? Where's my nurse?"

"They're all gone, Ma."

She blinked up at him, then down at the plastic ID band on her wrist. "What am I doing here?"

"You were a patient here. You had cancer."

"You *lie*."

"It's true, Ma. Twenty years ago."

"Oh," she said in a small child's voice. She let the flashlight slip to the floor, her veined and spotted hands going up to cover her face. Calhoun stood there for a moment, then put his arms around the round, broad haunch of her shoulders. Her hospital gown was as soft as his childhood pajamas, the one with the little breast pocket just big enough for a Matchbox car.

"Mm." She withdrew with a sniff. "Drinking again. I can smell it on you."

"Ma, please."

"Well, I suppose you come by it honestly."

"Leave Dad out of it."

"Your father?" She scowled, creating a little flesh-cushion between her eyebrows. "Drinking was the one thing he didn't do."

"But you always said . . ."

She smiled a sad sweet smile that kept her lips pressed together. "I know what I said."

Calhoun had never seen her smile like that.

"At first I was just lonely," she said. "He was never around for us. I'd have one before dinner and another when he didn't come home. And when he still didn't come home I just put the bottle by the couch."

"All that was *you?*" Calhoun asked. "All those bottles?"

"In the end it didn't matter how much I had, I could always smell her all over him, her cheap perfume and cigarettes. In the end, he didn't even try to hide it from me. The signs were everywhere."

"Ma—"

"He had the gall to tell me I was the one who needed help, can you imagine? After I sat up with you all those nights. *I took you to church!*" She jerked her head upward, throat tendons stretching the loose flesh in webs. "How you cried for him, Stevie, night after night, wanted him to come home. It got to the point where you couldn't sleep unless I . . ."

"Unless you what?"

"Nothing." She turned slowly around, dragging her IV pole on its squeaking wheels. Calhoun caught up to her.

"Unless you what, Ma?"

"I only gave you little sips," she said. "Just enough to make you sleepy. Some nights it took more than others."

"For how long?"

"Go ahead, blame your mother. That's the thing now, isn't it?"

"For how many nights, Ma?"

"Oh, so now it's my fault poor little Stevie needs to be drunk by sunset just to make it through the night." One crooked eyebrow, badly in need of plucking, arched up. "Poor little Stevie, tell yourself it's not your fault. Even if poor little Stevie had been sober tonight it wouldn't have mattered. That doctor would have taken his keys anyhow."

Calhoun shook his head. "What doctor?"

"Oh, please. Why do you think he wanted you in that room with him tonight, because you were so important?"

"Why would Dr. Walker take my keys?"

"You've always been the Judas goat. Why should tonight be any different? Dr. Walker has business with Frank Snow. He knew you'd be too drunk to stop him."

"What business?"

"What business? What business is there?" She grinned, lips splitting so Calhoun could count all her remaining teeth, two on the top, three on the bottom, and Calhoun realized that this wasn't his mother at all. It was a cruel imposter generated by this place, the hospital itself, product of the unholy union of tonight's events. When she spoke again, her voice was thick and suety. "The business between a man and a woman, the business between God and the devil, the business between the tree and the ax. Glork!"

Calhoun could only stare at her. It was what he'd been reduced to.

"It's okay, honey. You don't have to understand. Here." She slipped her hand into the pocket of her gown, brought out a flat unlabeled pint of something brown and translucent, and pressed it in his hand. "Mama make it all better."

"Put that away."

"Too good for it now?" She picked up the flashlight and shined it through the bottle. "Look closer."

Calhoun found himself staring helplessly into the brown liquid. At first he saw nothing. Then something shimmered inside its depths, coalesced, and took shape, utterly convincing in its verisimilitude, a tall man in a white coat.

Walker.

He had Calhoun's keys in one hand and a flashlight in the other. He was in the ER, locking the door. His mother was right. It had been Walker all along.

*You know that can't be right, it was Snow, he—*

That voice, urgent but still rational, was overwhelmed by a hot, sunburned feeling that crawled across his scalp, a feeling he was unaccustomed to managing, rage, yes, and a newfound sense of purpose.

He brought the bottle to his lips and took a long, burning drink.

## 35.

Flashlight balanced behind him, Mike pushed aside a stack of X-rays and lab reports and found a yellowed newspaper clipping in the bottom of the jacket.

He read the headline: "Miracle Boy" Comes Out of Coma.

He skimmed the first few paragraphs. After recapping the accident that had landed Snow in Pediatric ICU, the article told how the Pediatric ICU team had "heroically" brought the boy from "the very brink of death." The local reporter's efforts at journalistic objectivity hadn't lasted much longer than his opening sentences.

> "We got lucky with this one," one doctor, who spoke under conditions of anonymity, told this reporter yesterday. "Everyone here knew that the prognosis for this boy was not at all good. But this is a reminder that every once in a while, you win one."

And, farther down:

> The modesty of the Tanglewood staff hardly fits the facts of what happened to Franklin Snow. Other clinicians concur that, due to the horrific trauma of the accident, the boy's body had already ceased to function, and his odds of surviving, let alone staging this kind of dramatic recovery, were virtually zero. Already there is talk in medical circles of the ICU team's "miracle-worker" approach. . . .

As he put the article down, Mike noticed there was another part of the clipping, folded over backward. He lifted it up and stared at it for a long time.

It was a photo.

The right side of the picture showed a man that, Mike realized with a start, had to be Dr. Walker. Walker didn't just look thirty years younger: he looked an entire *lifetime* younger, his face fresh and bright without a single line on it. Whatever had passed through his life between then and now had done more than cut into Walker's face, it had completely reshaped its entire landscape into something infinitely older and more tired. Drained it.

But it wasn't Dr. Walker who held Mike's gaze. It was the small blond boy in the wheelchair to the left of him. The boy was wearing a hospital gown over a T-shirt with a rocket ship on it. The letters on the front of the rocket read "USA." The boy was smiling sweetly, giving the camera a cheerful thumbs-up.

Someone had drawn two red *X*'s over either of the little boy's eyes.

And underneath in the same red ink, was scrawled:

<u>BURNING IN HELL</u>

The flashlight caught the face of his watch. It was midnight. How had it gotten so late, so soon?

He heard a clicking sound from overhead.

Everywhere, all around him, the lights came back on.

## 36

**Dr. Walker squinted, eyes readapting,** vision coming back in painful bolts of white.

The power was back on.

Frank Snow was standing in front of him.

Without the prison jumpsuit, Walker might not have recognized him. Snow looked pale and strung-out, worse than when the ambulance had brought him here. He was leaning against the wall, sagging really, with blood in various degrees of dryness caked on his jumpsuit, striations of orange and red. Blood was running from his fingers where he'd cut them open.

"It's you."

"Hey," Snow murmured, put up his hands. "You got me."

Walker didn't move, didn't come any closer. "What do you want?"

"I'm done."

"Done?"

"With my preparations." Snow tried to spit on the floor but some of it stuck to his chin. He wiped it away with the back of his wrist, looking up at Walker with a hooked wire of a smile. "Here's your chance to be a hero. Always was your favorite part, wasn't it?"

"I don't follow."

"Sure you do." Snow reached down, tugged up the leg of his pants, and brought out a gun—*one of the cops' pistols*, Walker thought—holding it up by the barrel so Walker could see it. He set it on the floor and kicked it down the hall to Walker. "Go on, take it. It's loaded. Just make sure you take the safety off before you try to pull the trigger, otherwise you're liable to embarrass yourself. I know how you hate that."

"If you think I'm going to kill you—"

"One other thing. I got these, too, if that'll make you feel better." He withdrew a pair of police handcuffs from his other pant leg and held them up, snapped the metal bracelets on his own wrists, then drew the silver chain tight. "There, you're doubly safe now, right?"

"Why are you doing this?"

"Like I said, I'm finished. Everything's set in place. All the deals are on the table. What happens next is up to you."

"Me?"

"All of you."

"Where are the others?"

"Here and there."

"Alive?" Walker asked.

It couldn't quite be called a smile. "Most of them. For now."

"What's that supposed to mean?"

"You'll see."

Walker bent down and picked up the gun, looked at it in his hand. "What did you mean, everything's set in place?"

Snow tilted his head back and stared up at the ceiling for a long time, as if there were something there that interested him a great deal. When he looked back at Walker his eyes were thoughtful but not distracted; if anything, they focused on Walker with an intensity that unsettled him deeply.

"Everybody these days talks a lot about freedom," Snow said, "free will, civil liberty, the right to choose. What a crock of shit." He spat again, this time clearing his chin, hitting the floor. Walker thought it looked pink with blood. "The fact is that ninety-nine percent of you are nothing but a bunch of slaves. From the day you're born to the day you die, this whole world isn't anything but chains around your feet and doors you ain't ever going to unlock." His voice rose, a mocking falsetto: *"Do we have your keys?"*

"You're not making any sense."

"Take that gun in your hand. You're already wishing you never picked it up. It doesn't feel right. But I gave it to you, so you took it. Protector of life, physician, healer," he snorted, "you're just a slave to your baser impulses, Doc— routines, habits, just like everybody else."

"So what's your game?"

"You tell me. You're the one who brought me back here tonight. How come?"

"You know why. To undo what I did," Walker said. "Thirty years ago."

Snow gazed at him coldly. "That's not possible."

"I have to try."

"See, that's exactly what I mean. You and all the rest, running in the same dumb circles your whole life, jumping at every noise, fumbling for the light switch since the day you were born. Trying to make things better, always making them worse, never knowing why, getting more and more turned around until somebody finally puts you out of your misery."

"You're referring to yourself, I suppose?" Walker asked.

"Not exactly. I always gave every one of them a choice."

"Doesn't make you any less of a monster."

"Only a monster?" Snow's eyebrows shot up in what appeared to be genuine disbelief. "Come on, Doc, you of all people ought to know better than that."

Walker measured him, felt Snow's leaden gaze resting on him. He took a breath and let it out. Snow was right about one thing. However much he might think he was free to choose, when it came to some aspects of his life, he had always known only one way to end this. Everything that had happened since Snow's arrival here thirty years ago hadn't altered that fundamental truth.

"I'm taking you back upstairs," Walker said. "To the sixth floor."

Snow appeared supremely unsurprised. "By elevator?"

"We'll walk."

"Tell you the truth, I'm not sure I can climb stairs, shape I'm in."

"Try."

"Sure."

By the time they reached the room on the sixth floor, Snow was pale, forehead dripping with sweat. A thin trickle of scarlet dribbled from one nostril.

"Well, look at this," he said, out of breath. "Right back where we started, huh? What's your next move?"

"I'm not sure what went wrong before, but I'm reopening the hole," Walker said. "And sticking you back down into it, permanently."

"Think you can do it without the book?"

"Get on your knees."

"You're an old man, Doc."

"I said get on your knees."

"Anything you say." Snow wiped his nose, put his back to the wall, and sank to the floor. "I got the best seat in the house right here. I'm just going to sit right back and watch it unfold."

He sat quietly, cuffed hands between his knees, gazing placidly up at Walker. The doctor didn't look back at him. He could almost feel Snow's smile on the back of his head.

He had to do this. But for the first time in his life he already knew he was going to fail.

# 37.

Jolie woke to an inner alarm that seemed to emanate from the small bones inside her face. Her head ached badly and her first thought was: hangover, the worst of her life. Her muscles felt weak and there was too much tightness inside her skull, not enough in the rest of her body. Maybe if she lay here long enough without moving, the pressure would equalize.

*Five more minutes, Mom, please?*

Then she realized the buzzing was coming from the fluorescent lights overhead, and it all came back to her in a sudden, unpleasant rush.

She was lying in the fourth-floor hallway, up in the psychiatric ward, half-curled and shivering. In light of what she'd just remembered, two previously unremarkable facts took on critical importance.

The power was back on.

And she was alive.

Inside her cheek, there was some kind of cut. Her thoughts flashed to the drill that Snow had stuck in her mouth while she clung to the fence. Why hadn't he killed her?

What time was it?

She'd never worn a watch, being one of those people who always seemed to know intuitively what time it was down to the minute. Now, though, she had no sense of the hour—day, night—or how long she'd been lying here. Standing up, testing her joints, she put her hands on the small of her back, stretched, and felt something crackle in her back pocket.

She pulled it out.

It was a folded sheet of yellow legal paper.

Opening it, she saw spidery child's handwriting, the same writing on the map that Snow had tried to smuggle into the hospital.

*You have a choice.  If you want to get out, do everything exactly as I say WITH-OUT EXCEPTION and you'll live to see daylight.  Follow the signs and remember, I could have killed you already.*

Follow the signs? She looked around, not expecting to see anything and at first she didn't. She reread the note. Snow clearly must have stuck it in her pocket when she was unconscious, and left her here to find it. But where was Snow?

*Follow the signs.*

At the end of the hall, painted on the wall in three bright-red smeary letters that could only be one thing, was the single word:

## OUT

with an arrow pointing to the right, down the back stairs.

*A trap. It's got to be.*

But that didn't make sense. Mad as it sounded, Snow was right: he could have already killed her, could have done whatever he wanted, including tying her up and torturing her, raping her. Instead he'd left her, unrestrained, fully clothed, relatively unmolested except for the cut inside her mouth and the note in her pocket. That had always been his trademark, she remembered, the notes. And the bargains.

Suppose he really was going to let her go free?

Jolie started walking toward the arrow.

## 38

Lights?

In the corner of the MRI suite, Sarah straightened her shoulders, feeling excruciatingly exposed, as if someone had yanked away a cloak that had been covering her. She'd been holding Eli on her lap in the near-darkness. He was fast asleep in her arms. When the power shuddered back on, her first thought was to look by the doorway, where she almost expected to see someone—*Mike? Snow?*—with one hand on the light switch.

But, of course, no one was there.

Why were the lights coming back on now, of all times?

She glanced at her cell phone. The screen told her it was midnight. There was still no signal. In her arms, Eli stirred but didn't open his eyes, sweaty and mired in the slow-motion violence of the hopelessly exhausted. He was sticky and hot, the fabric of his shirt rippled against his skin, his hair matted to the sides of his face, dark with perspiration. Even though he was in deep unconsciousness, his hands clutched hers with furious dedication, and in his slumber he mouthed a word:

*Snowman.*

That was when she noticed the mark on the back of his neck.

It began just beneath the base of his skull. What she'd first taken as a patch of sweaty hair was actually a black line rising up from his collar. Sarah tugged his shirt open and looked at his skin.

Every inch of his body between waist and neck was covered in writing.

Peeling his shirt off completely, the boy still not waking, Sarah held Eli at arm's length to examine the scrawls of inexpert black marker crawling over her son's chest and back, his nipples, shoulder blades, belly. It took her several minutes to put together what at first looked like a random crowd of words.

> *I told you I would let you out and I will. If you want to live to see daylight, fol-*
> *low the flag. Fail and you and the ones you love most will die in here slowly and*
> *in worse ways than you can possibly imagine. Remember, I could have killed*
> *your son but didn't.*
> Snowman

She was still reading when Eli grunted, crossed his arms over his bare chest, shivering. Sarah barely noticed, too preoccupied by what she saw. When had Snow done this? *Obviously, when the two of us were separated.* She hadn't noticed until now without the benefit of any light. The thought of Snow taking off Eli's shirt and writing on him . . .

*Don't think about it.*

But she had to think about it. It was all she *could* think about. That's why he'd left it there, for her to consider. Follow the flag?

Eli's eyes opened blearily. "Mommy? I dreamed . . ." His voice fading as he realized he hadn't been dreaming, arms clutching her tightly. "What's going on?"

Could she say "I don't know" one more time and have it mean anything? What else was she supposed to say?

"Honey, do you remember someone writing on you?"

"Writing?"

"On your skin."

Eli scowled down at his chest, eyes still scrunched with sleepiness. He shook his head, then paused and nodded.

"Did he do anything else? Hurt you, or . . . ?"

He shook his head again, less certain now. Even as he did so, she saw him running his hands down his arms, cupping his elbows as if ensuring he hadn't sustained any other injury. "Mommy? Can you put my shirt back on? I'm cold."

She slid it back over his head, mindful of the lump on his forehead, and saw him wince with pain. After all of this, his worst wound of the night still came from a moment when she hadn't been paying close enough attention.

"Did the man who did this say anything to you about a flag?"

"No," he mumbled, eyelids heavy. He was already tilting toward her, wanting her to hold him so he could go back to sleep.

Sarah held him. How much did she want to take Eli somewhere and scrub these horrible words off his skin? In a strange way, seeing them in normal light made her more afraid than ever to make a move, feeling like Snow was watching her, knowing she had to comply.

*When the time comes, all you'll have to do is follow the signs.*

Suddenly everything clicked—the locked doors and darkness, the taunting voice on the radio, the corpses in the dark. Six hours ago, all she had was the note Jolie had written to Mike, along with a receipt from her husband's pocket for a diamond bracelet they couldn't afford, a style she never wore, and the terrible knowledge that he was cheating on her again. Since then Frank Snow had taught her about true fear, and fear had cleared her mind, reset her counters, and filed her instincts down to hair-trigger sensitivity.

After rocking Eli back and forth for a moment she fell still, her ears picking up the sound of static. It came from one of the cabinets across the suite. She stood up, the boy's head resting on her shoulder, and walked to the sink, opened the cupboard door, and saw the radio on the shelf. It was switched on, broadcasting nothing.

She pushed the button. "Hello?"

Eli squirmed, grumbled; she sensed him listening in his half-waking way. But there was no answer, and she wasn't surprised. If Snow was playing games, she could hardly expect anything as coherent as a conversation.

But there *was* something, very faint, in the background, a sound she didn't recognize until she heard Eli imitating it, a muffled metallic clanging through the radio's speaker. Sarah looked at him.

"What is it?"

"The flag," he said, still half-asleep.

"What?"

"When we came in," Eli said. "Remember? *Clang-clang.* The flag?"

"By the emergency room entrance? Is that where?"

Eli nodded, so weary, rested his head back down.

*Follow the flag.*

Sarah started moving.

# 39.

**Calhoun opened his eyes.** The latest version of his mind felt like it had a rusty steel pipe slammed through it, his tongue pasted like desert roadkill to the roof of his mouth, all very familiar sensations from years of chronic binge drinking. He burped, triggering dyspeptic burning in his belly and chest. The bottle on the floor next to him was empty.

*All of it?*

The lights were back on.

Calhoun groaned, clutched his temples. To his beleaguered brain and eyes, having the lights back wasn't necessarily an improvement, but it did allow him to see what he'd missed about the bottle.

It wasn't *completely* empty.

There was a rolled-up piece of paper stuck inside it, the damp lower edge tinged brown with the dregs of the bourbon that had been the bottle's original occupant. He'd gotten the bourbon from his mother, the omnipresent Marilyn Lawrence Calhoun. The only problem with that scenario was that Marilyn Lawrence Calhoun had been dead for twenty years.

*So you had a bottle stashed up here somewhere for yourself and you forgot about it. You blacked out, took some of that short-term memory with you. Imagine that.*

Hand trembling, he picked up the bottle and studied it. His mother had said some things to him that he hadn't believed then and couldn't believe now, though he sensed they were probably the truth. More often than not, the truth turned out to be what you couldn't accept the first time around.

He turned the bottle upside down and shook it, then gave up and flung it as hard as he could at the wall. The glass shattered and the note fell out.

He read it once, pinched it into a ball, and stuffed it into his pocket.

Suddenly his headache was gone.

## 40

Mike stepped out of the file room and stopped dead in his tracks, staring at the giant red arrow painted on the wall in front of him. The arrow pointed right. Above it, in wide-set capitals, was slashed the word:

<u>OUT</u>

*One arrow,* he thought, *one word, underlined. But how much sense does it make to follow directions written in blood?*

He could see down the hall where it pointed. Likewise empty. And down at the end was another arrow, pointing left. Is this what Snow had been doing while the lights were out, redecorating the hospital with dubious directions or misdirections, signposts to certain doom? Creating a maze that led deeper into the guts of the building for the simple purpose of stringing them along for the rest of the night?

It struck Mike as a very real possibility. Wherever "OUT" was, he wouldn't have been surprised to find Snow waiting for him there with a machete, or bone autopsy saw, or worse.

But he wasn't there yet.

He walked to the second arrow, peered around the corner, saw another empty hall. With the lights back on, these surroundings ought to have felt familiar again, even comforting. But something about them had inexplicably changed, like debris left behind by retreating floodwaters, altering the landscape, rendering it permanently alien.

The next arrow pointed at a stairway door.

Mike stopped and looked at it. Opening that door without knowing what was behind it could very well be the definition of stupidity. *Open it up and the monster pops out, Wes Craven 101.*

No, for the time being at least, he was perfectly willing to—

Footsteps.

He started backing away through what felt like invisible quicksand. And the quicksand was inside and outside his legs, slowing him down in two ways. Too late he realized that his response time, already conditioned to darkness and the thousands of incidental hiding places it had created, had now been fatally compromised by the relentless omnipresence of the light. Footsteps louder now, the door flying open—

Jolie bursting out, spilling into his arms, already ready to scream.

"Whoa." He caught her shoulders. "Jo, it's Mike. It's okay."

She was breathing hard, big asthmatic whoops that made her shoulders leap, eyes oval.

"Are you all right?"

"Mike . . . I thought . . . thought you were . . ." The tiny hardened buckshot of her pupils twitched to the arrow up the hall, voice high and unnatural: "He marked the walls down here, too?"

"Yeah," he said. "I wasn't sure whether I should be following them or not."

"He said if we do what he wants, we'll survive."

"Snow told you that?"

"He wrote it, right here." Jolie took a piece of paper from her pocket and held it up. "See?"

Mike had to take the note himself. Her hand was shaking too much to allow him to make out the words. But the handwriting was what got him more than anything, the clumsy, inexperienced scrawl trying to carry the adult syntax. He thought of the picture he'd seen in the file room, the little boy in the USA sweater, giving a sweet, enthusiastic thumbs-up to the newspaper photographer. When Mike finished reading the note a third time, he handed it back to her, wanting to wipe off his hands.

"Where did you get this?" he asked.

"It was in my hip pocket when I woke up. He must have put it there. Did you get one?"

"No, I—" But his hand was already reaching back to his own pocket, fingers locating a barely perceptible bulge, and his voice died. He felt the blood drain from his cheeks as he pulled forth a small piece of paper, unreality hitting him like a breath of pure helium as he fumbled the sheet open.

*You have a choice. If you want out, go to the fire extinguisher at the end of the ground floor hall by the east elevator and look inside. Follow my instructions WITHOUT EXCEPTION and you will live. Remember, instead of giving you this note, I could have done things to you that would make the fires of hell look inviting by comparison.*

"When . . . ?"

Then he remembered back to the ER, when the hand had brushed up against him, even before the lights had gone out. Had he really been walking around with this note in his pocket since then? When else had Snow been that close to him?

*Anytime,* a deathly calm voice answered. *Anytime he wanted, in the dark.*

"I know the spot he's talking about," Jolie said, reading over his shoulder. "What do you think is there?"

Mike felt queasy. "No idea."

"We have to go find out."

All he had were questions, but he found himself nodding along anyway. Despite what Snow had written, they didn't really have a choice, did they?

No.

They walked up the hall, Mike realizing they were following the arrows again. He could see now how Snow had used the darkness to take absolute possession of the hospital, and them with it, remaking it in his own image. It was so simple—just a few hours in complete darkness in which to work, and the place was his.

*The familiar made unfamiliar. Uncanny.*

He saw the reception desk and the elevator. The fire extinguisher compartment was closed, looked untouched.

*What are you waiting for?*

He opened it. Inside, lodged next to the fire extinguisher, was a small bundle. Mike recognized the paper. It was another faded page of bootleg prison porn, like the one Snow had used to send him his first note back in MRI. The object wrapped inside the page was Jolie's digital camera.

"I don't get it," he said.

"Flip it over." Jolie pointed. "There's something written here."

Scrawled across the images of naked bodies, women and women, women and men, bare legs tangled together, dyed blond hair, painted lips, drug-dead eyes, were several slanting lines of writing:

*Pick a position. Take a picture. You and Jolie. Deliver the camera up to the Six East nurse's station, Pediatric Intensive Care, and leave it there on the desk. If your snapshot is good enough you'll get out alive.*

Mike shook his head. "This doesn't . . ." Looking around for surveillance cameras, seeing none, he turned to her. "How did he know we would both be here?"

"He sent me back down here, remember?" Jolie pointed. "The arrows? He wanted me here with you when you found it."

"This is crazy. He actually expects us to do this?"

She said nothing. Mike felt some numb part of him holding its breath, still expecting her to announce that somehow after all of this, she was kidding, ha-ha, it's all a big joke. But she just gazed back at him with the dead eyes of a prison camp detainee, a face he didn't want to look at. The only other place to direct his eyes was at the note written over the naked bodies and he definitely didn't want to look at that, either.

"I don't believe him," he said finally. Next to him, she was already peeling off her scrub top. "Wait a second, what are you doing?"

"What he wants." She jabbed one finger at the photos on the page, somehow even more garish and lurid for their worn-out condition, polished by hundreds of sets of hungry eyes. "That one, just do it and take the picture."

"Jolie, I'm not—"

"Your wife already thinks we're doing it anyway."

"He can't make us—"

"*Yes he can!*" she screamed and her hand swung out to slap him, hard, across the face. Mike felt the imprint of her palm rise over his cheek. She was crying, voice a rockslide of ugly black shale. "What, you're so afraid of being humiliated? You know what he did to me? He shoved a fucking drill in my mouth and made me suck it! I thought I was going to die!"

"Jolie—"

"Don't you get it yet?" She shoved him back against the wall. "I don't care what your fucking wife and child think! If humiliating you gets me out of here, you're doing it with me! *You are doing this with me!*"

It ended when Mike took the camera from her hand. She let him take it, but stared back at him with red-rimmed eyes, face grim and shining, expression set in stone.

## 41

**The ER waiting room was a lake of blood.** Eli, in her arms, was not awake to see it, a small mercy for which Sarah was still grateful. In the center, a stretcher lay on its side. She tried not to think about whose blood it might have been. But trying not to think about it didn't do her much good in the end.

She went to the ER exit, tested it, already bracing for disappointment.

Still locked.

She listened for the clang of the flagpole outside, but she heard nothing other than the hospital's climate-control systems doing their job, big ventilation fans playing catch-up, recycling the air now that the power was back on. Now more than ever she hated white noise. It wasn't just noise pollution, it was sonic camouflage, hiding the sounds of who knew what?

She wondered if she'd misinterpreted Snow's message. Was he simply tormenting her? The darkness may have conditioned her to follow his requests, but Frank Snow was undoubtedly crazy, and because he was crazy, his games could very easily amount to nothing, a gleeful series of clues that culminated with her careening straight off a cliff. In a way she actually preferred the darkness, where at least there was no illusion of structure or—

Then she saw it.

The colors caught her eye from twenty feet away, a miniature American flag like the kind they sold at the hospital gift shop. At first she thought it was just lying on the floor. Then, coming closer, getting a better angle, she saw its wooden stick was lodged in the doors of a waiting elevator. The doors tried to close on the stick, reopened, tried to close, reopened, over and over.

*Follow the flag.*

She carried Eli up the hall, nudged the wooden stick aside, craned her neck for a better look.

The elevator was empty.

Almost.

There was a pistol lying in the corner, like the one she'd seen McPhee carrying. Written above it, on the wall, in red:

<u>For you</u>

Sarah stepped inside. On the keypad, a red circle had been slashed around the number six.

She pushed it. The doors slid shut.

On the way up, she picked up the gun.

**Calhoun saw everything.** He glimpsed it only briefly, a landscape chiseled by a momentary flash of lightning, but the flash was revelatory, a coruscating moment of clarity.

It happened as he was running up the stairs, somewhere between the fifth and sixth floors. He felt supercharged now, a smooth-running gun. This newfound energy was nothing but good, cocaine-good, high-grade, high-test, first-class, prime-rib American good. Young or old, drunk or sober, he'd never felt this good on the best day of his life. Some part of him knew what it meant.

The hospital was coming alive inside him.

This realization paid dividends directly into his bloodstream, running its systems straight to his brain. In a blink he saw its miles of hallways, rooms, doors, and blind windows, every glittering inch like a circuit board he himself had designed. He glimpsed beauty in its complexity, the only true beauty, like a battlefield where countless thousands had given their lives. The immensity of death's pattern made jewelry of the air, a shimmering web whose residue lingered on his cheeks and forehead like mask after mask after mask.

At the top of the stairs he stopped.

They were all staring at him.

Mike and Sarah and their little boy, Dr. Walker, Jolie, and Frank Snow himself, all were here. Through his shock, some ageless, intuitive part of Calhoun saw them for what they truly were, beings that had preceded humanity in this place, primordial things, beings older than the planet's own measurement of time. He had interrupted something primal among them and now they gazed down at him from a place he'd never dreamed of, not even when he'd been locked in that room with Snow earlier.

Calhoun took a step forward, unable to look away.

They were playing with something round, and after a moment he realized it was the severed head of one of the policemen. The pale cheeks were wet from a still-bubbling kettle that sat on the floor behind them. One of the eyes had fallen out.

Mike tossed the head and the little boy, Eli, bent over backward on his hands and scuttled after it, mewling like a cat. Turning to Calhoun, Mike opened his mouth as if to speak, but all that came out was a roar, a compendium of humming wires, ventilation fans, and the thump of compressors: the voice of the hospital itself. Somehow what was left of his lips shaped these noises until Calhoun recognized the words clearly enough.

*Do we have your keys?*

Calhoun's expression must have been answer enough. The party erupted in silent laughter. It was a fine joke. They were free, and he was trapped, all because he had lost his keys. Calhoun felt his previous strength curdle into a melted Styrofoam cup of self-loathing. He was a drunk, a hopeless walking abortion of a man from whom almost nothing was expected, charged with the most mundane of tasks. Yet he had somehow managed to lose his keys on the one night where having his keys meant everything.

*No! Walker took them from me!*

*Not true,* a mournful voice replied. *It was his fault, all of it, only his—*

"That's not right." He forced himself to stare at the strange party on the landing. "The son of a bitch took them from me. He set me up here. I don't know why but it's not my fault. Wherever you all came from, he was the one who let you out. He started this. You're here, all of you, because of him, not me. I'm going to get my keys back and then I'm getting the fuck out of here."

The group regarded him flatly, already losing interest. The thing that had disguised itself as Sarah picked up the cop's head and began tossing it in the air. When the boy leaped up and tried to grab it from her she clubbed him with her elbow and took an enormous proprietary bite from the skull, grinning at Calhoun in a way that made him wish he'd never been born. He could hear her chewing. It sounded like someone eating broken glass.

One by one they faded from view.

Calhoun could actually feel them vanishing back inside what remained of his mind. He knew everything now: the hospital was alive. He was trapped inside it, but it was inside him, too. That was the hell of it. Everything, every fucking thing, was wrong with this picture, and guilty or not, he would do whatever it took to escape from it. Even rats knew when to abandon ship, and he and pride hadn't been on speaking terms for a long, long time.

*Even so, it's too late. It's inside you, too. You've been bought and paid for.*

Except Snow had provided him with a way out, hadn't he? In his note in the whiskey bottle he had told Calhoun where to go and exactly what to do and Calhoun intended to follow those instructions to the letter. Could he trust him? Did it matter?

No. Even if it meant throwing away every scrap of what made him human, sacrificing his soul itself . . . nothing was going to stop him from getting out of here.

With that in mind he went through the door to the sixth floor and into Pediatric Intensive Care.

Mike and Jolie arrived at the nurse's station on the sixth floor, Pediatric ICU, neither of them speaking. The air still stunk of unnatural smoke and ash. Jolie coughed but said nothing. Except for the fabric-on-fabric out-of-synch shuffle of their footsteps, they traveled in absolute silence, not meeting each other's eyes.

There was a bloody circle drawn on the top of the nurses' desk. Mike set the camera inside the circle.

Jolie cleared her throat. "Look."

He glanced up, unable to do otherwise. The smoke-stained wall above the station was slashed with two red arrows pointing in opposite directions.

One pointed to the right. It was marked *M*.

The other, marked *J*, pointed left.

"I guess this is where we part company," Jolie said.

"Maybe—" Mike began, and stopped. She was already turning left to follow her arrow up the hall, moving like a child's idea of a robot, a stiff-jointed thing whose outward humanity only made it scary and sad. Halfway down the hall Mike saw her pause and look back with a forlorn glance. Then she pivoted to face a chair pushed up against the wall. There must have been something written there, some instruction waiting for her, because she abruptly turned again and sat down in the chair. That was the first time in this most recent visit to the sixth floor that Mike felt a deep dose of sensory distortion ripple through his vision. The air wobbled around him like heat on a desert highway: seasick. His mouth, bone-dry just a moment earlier, was now salivating so excessively he almost had to spit.

Instead he turned right and shambled on his way, feeling more than slightly unsteady on his feet. He could already tell he was breathing too quickly, not deep enough, and forced himself to pay attention to his respiration. He'd traveled only a dozen paces, perhaps less, when he stopped again.

Lying on the floor in front of him was a book. It looked very old, bound in leather or sheepskin with the stiff yellow pages bristling unevenly out the sides. It also looked heavy. There was no writing on the cover, nothing to indicate front from back.

A note protruded out of the top. He pulled it clear.

*Take this to the hospital operators' office. Turn on the hospital intercom and read the marked page aloud. Do this and you and your family will be allowed to live. Fail me and you will all die, starting with your wife.*

Mike opened the book to where the note had been sticking out. Molecular chains of letters marched from one edge of the page to the other, definitely not English. Some of the letters he recognized but others were symbols, pictographs, somewhere between cave etchings and Cyrillic characters. They swam before his eyes. How the hell was he supposed to read this?

He looked again.

The page was in Latin.

He looked again.

The page was in runic.

He looked again.

The page was blank.

Except it wasn't, quite. There were pictures, a view of a small boy in a hospital bed with a breathing tube in his throat. A man in a white coat stood over him, clutching something that went to work directly on Mike's gnawed-down sanity.

He slapped the book shut and flung it as hard as he could at the wall, the binding cracking, making a little indentation there as loose pages spilled across the carpeted floor. Seeing the thing fall apart cleared his head. Kicking it made him feel even better. Was Snow watching this? *Let him watch.* He hoped Snow could hear him, too. "You know what I'm going to do, you son of a bitch? I'm going to find my wife and kid and we're walking out of here. How do you like that?"

No response, of course, and had he expected one? It didn't matter. He knew where he needed to go. The realization was just there, that was how he knew he'd earned it, how he knew it was right.

He ran back up the hall to the rotunda, where the other hallway branched off, retracing the route where he and Walker had rushed Snow earlier in the evening. The frozen flow of smoke damage marbled the walls, a permanent addition, like the skins of so many ghosts. Up ahead he could already see the door that Calhoun and the doctor had taken Snow through just before the explosion. It was open. He got to the end of the corridor, turned the corner, went through the door—

And stopped.

Because this couldn't be right.

He was in the hospital operators' room.

*Impossible! It's on a completely different level of the hospital, down on the main floor! That smoke from before, it's still stuck in my lungs, making me see things—*

The physical reality of his surroundings defied any further attempt at rationalization. Long tidy tables flanked either side with a dozen empty chairs in front of a dozen phones, computer consoles, and microphones. Muted light emanated from the fixtures overhead with an almost audible sigh. Mike stared at it, turned to look back.

The door clicked shut behind him.

It wasn't until he looked at the tables a second time that he saw the book there, resting next to the microphone closest to him. Its binding was intact, its pages all there, as before, waiting for him. Even the chair had been pulled back slightly, an unspoken invitation.

One by one, the phones began to chime.

Sarah stepped out of the elevator with the pistol in one hand and her son in the other, a combination she'd never imagined for herself. But it was a night of firsts, wasn't it?

The elevator doors had opened on the sixth-floor rotunda with a big semi-circular nursing station in the middle. Up ahead she saw two arrows drawn on the wall, pointing two different ways, marked *J* and *M*.

"Look at the camera," a distant voice said from up the hall.

Sarah turned in the direction of the voice. Far down at the end of the corridor, looking like a trick of perspective, Alice through the looking glass, Jolie was sitting in a chair. She was staring at the wall in front of her, not looking over.

"Jolie?" Sarah said. "What's—"

"Look at the camera."

"Where's Mike?"

"Look at the camera."

Sarah's first thought was a surveillance camera, but then she saw the little silver camera sitting on the counter in front of her in a ring of blood. She rested Eli on the counter, away from the blood, keeping one arm draped on his waist and allowing his deep-sleeping weight to rest against her as she picked up the camera.

"Did something happen?" she asked. "Is Snow making you do this?"

Jolie just kept staring at the wall. Sarah found the blood-encrusted power button, tapped it on. Images lit the screen and she clicked through them, photos of empty hallways, vacant doorways and hospital walls, shadows that made no sense. Was there a story here?

Click: an open space surrounded in chain-link fence.

Click: an orange jumpsuit blazing faster than the shutter could capture it.

Click: Jolie's face blown up in a silent scream.

Click: even closer, just half her mouth and one open eye.

Click, click, click.

"What's he showing me?" Sarah asked. "What am I supposed to—"

Click.

She stared at the last image on the screen. It was a blurry close-up of two bodies twisted around each other, the pornographic equivalent of a crime-scene photo. She saw flesh, knees, body hair, little else. Sex? Only by the most generous of standards. A dead man's heart had more passion in it than this.

"Who is this?"

Jolie, in her chair, didn't answer.

"Who are these people?"

She was still looking at the picture when the man rose up from behind the desk with his hand around Eli's throat. It was the security guard, Calhoun. His face was full of broken clockwork, voice an atonal buzz.

"You're coming with me."

Sarah looked for the pistol where she'd laid it on the counter. It was already gone. The gun was in Calhoun's hand. He rested the barrel against Eli's temple, just below the swollen knot in the boy's forehead.

"Now."

"What are you doing?"

"Trading your son for my keys."

"*What?*"

"My deal, the one he offered me." Calhoun pulled something from his pocket, a balled-up note, flicked it past her off the counter, where it fell to the floor. Sarah never took her eyes off Eli.

"I'm getting out of here," Calhoun said. "You try to stop me, I'll shoot him. Give me any resistance, I'll shoot him. We clear?" He had already scooped the sleeping boy up in one arm, the pistol barrel not budging as he walked back up the hall. Sarah followed, the smoke-damaged walls growing blacker and more intense around them, Hiroshima wallpaper that obviated any remaining institutional neutrality the place might have had. She felt her own thoughts shifting, becoming unfamiliar to her as some subtle outside presence took hold.

"Did he tell you to do this?" she asked. "Because you don't have to do this. We can all get out of here together."

Calhoun didn't even look back. At the end of the hall, he stopped in front of a narrow doorway Sarah hadn't noticed until they were right in front of it.

"I brought him like you asked." Calhoun's voice was drab and monochromatic as he spoke through the doorway to whoever was inside. "Now give me what's mine."

Sarah peered over Calhoun's shoulder, into the depths of the room. At first all she saw was black—not darkness, but the scorched and peeling planks of the walls and ceiling. Every surface glowered with barely subdued heat. A burned stuffed animal lay in the corner, the charred remains of a child's hospital bed off to one side. In the center of the room a ragged hole in the floor dropped down to nowhere.

Next to the hole, Dr. Walker was standing over a man in a prison uniform.

"Calhoun?" Walker jerked his head up at the security guard, then toward Sarah. He looked like a man whose worst fears were being confirmed before his very eyes. "What are you doing here?"

No one said anything. Having looked into the face of the man kneeling on the floor, Sarah discovered that she couldn't avert her stare. It was Snow, she thought, it had to be. Adrift in his orange jumpsuit, he slouched on the floor in handcuffs, a partially melted wax model of menace. Blankness had made taxidermist's marbles of his eyes. The only remaining trace of life in his face was his grin, but it was real enough, she thought, more than real, it was alive, seeming to quiver supernaturally in the air.

"You all need to get out of here, now." Walker flicked a quick glance at Sarah. "Especially you. What's happening here doesn't concern you."

"That's fine." Sarah looked at Calhoun. "Give me back my son."

"No, see, that ain't part of my deal." Calhoun took a step back, moved the gun from Eli to Walker. "You took my keys, Doc. I want 'em back."

Walker's voice, high and trembling: "I don't have—"

"Yeah? How about I shake your coat pockets, see what rattles out?"

"Don't come any closer!"

"Fuck it then. I'm ready to kill both of you dead right now."

"Give me my child," Sarah said.

"Bitch, you are gonna shut the fuck up." Calhoun clutched Eli tighter, the gun back on the boy's head. "I've got one ticket out of here and I'm using it." And to Walker: "Keys, now, asshole, before I start killing people."

"Who told you—" Walker started and cut himself off, staring down at Snow. "I should've known."

Calhoun glared at him. "What the hell are you talking about?"

"He's playing us against each other."

"Yeah, well, I've had about a bellyful of being played with." The pistol barrel slid over the bump on Eli's forehead and Sarah saw the boy flinch, trying in vain to seek out some chamber of sleep where the pain couldn't reach him. "Talk, now."

"Stop it!" Sarah felt the emergency switch trigger in her brain, the circuit breaker blowing its cabinet door wide open. "For God's sake, if you have his keys, give them back!"

Walker still didn't say anything for what felt like whole minutes. Finally, he put his hand in his pocket and took out a ring of keys, handing them to Calhoun.

Taking his keys back, Calhoun actually appeared to change, not metaphorically but in actual physicality. It was only subtle for the first few moments, and then the alteration became frighteningly obvious. Time-lapse flowers, bright as poppies, blossomed in his cheeks, spreading scarlet through his pigmentation until even his irises reddened, thickened, maddened in their sockets. Invisible hooks drew the corners of his mouth down into what still technically should have been called a grin. Leaning forward, he inhaled deeply through his nose as if memorizing the scent of the room to file away for future reference.

"They're useless, you know," Walker said. "No better to you now than the gun in your hand."

"Is that a fact." Calhoun's voice had changed, too, thickened somehow. "We'll see about that when I shoot this piece of shit dead."

Walker shook his head. "Frank Snow's already dead," he said. "He's been dead for years."

Mike lifted the book's heavy cover, flipping pages until he reached the picture he'd seen before, the one that had made him slap the book shut: the little boy with the breathing tube and the man in the white coat standing over him.

No question, the little boy was the same one he'd seen in the newspaper photo, corn-silk hair with the USA sweater, Frank Snow. The white-coated man was a 1973 version of Dr. Walker, younger, immeasurably younger. Walker wasn't looking at the boy. He was clutching something in his hands, something Mike couldn't see from here, until—

The image inside the book tilted, shifting into three dimensions, the room angling as in a mirror, and Mike felt the amusement park vertigo of toppling forward into unexpected depths. He wasn't looking at the hospital room anymore but somewhere else, the boundaries of his body dissolving into a fine mist, drifting through the page into a bright rectangle of cool air.

In front of him now, the steering wheel of a car with a windshield above it, cruising through the wooded autumn countryside. There was the smell of apples and dry hay, the sky blue and clear for miles in all directions. Soft jazz played on the car radio, a trumpet he somehow knew was being manipulated by someone named Art Farmer.

The road curved and through a clearing he saw a farmhouse with cars parked out in front. None of the cars looked like they had rolled off the assembly line after the mid-seventies. A sign out in front of the barn read: ESTATE SALE TODAY.

The car stopped and Mike felt himself getting out. That was the first time he realized that the body that his consciousness had settled back into was not his own. The hands, while masculine, were too slender, the fingers too long and agile to be his. As he crossed the lawn to the house, his pace was smooth and confident, almost as if he were gliding rather than walking. Up ahead, two men in overalls were lugging a vanity down the front steps and he saw a flash of himself in the mirror. The face of Dr. Walker, the younger Walker, gazed back at him from the mirror's depths.

*I don't want to go in there.*

Not a choice: he was inside the book now, a prisoner of its pages, seeing what it wanted him to see. Entering the old farmhouse, moving among the men and women examining the items for sale, he was already ascending the stairs. His gaze hovered here and there, an old chair, a painting of an elderly woman, floating from room to room but never lingering longer than a moment.

In the corner bedroom, one of Walker's slender hands reached out to examine the workmanship of a Shaker headboard. It pulled the headboard forward and something fell out from behind it, an object that had been trapped behind the bed and the wall.

The point of view swam down for a better look.

It was the leather-bound book. Mike saw Dr. Walker's beautiful smooth hands lifting it, brushing off dust and dried spider carcasses, opening it to scan pages of faded writing.

*Put it down!*

It was too late. He was already downstairs, paying for the book, carrying it back to his car.

Here a big chunk of the footage was missing. The images came quicker after that, spliced erratically.

Inside the hospital: paramedics rushing in with the boy on a stretcher. Frank Snow, three years old, motor vehicle accident, no other survivors. Walker's point of view came jostling forward into a field of intense lights, the hands moving expertly to cut away the boy's shirt, taking stock of multiple injuries, the small body hardly big enough to contain all the things wrong with it. Turning to give orders, swiveling back to concentrate on the boy. Sudden spurt of blood coming from the boy's mouth, so much blood—

A dark study illuminated solely by a desk lamp, very late at night. A cup of coffee and the leather-bound book, Walker's finger tracing lines of text. In the background, the steady, somehow unbearable tick of a clock.

Later: a narrow hospital room, the boy in bandages amid a forest of IV drips and a breathing tube down his throat; motionless, eyes half-closed. A yellow line charting his heart rhythms.

Later still. Walker's hands scribbling notes in a chart, the handwriting from Snow's file. Writing faster, the tip of the pen gouging the paper. A signature slashed on an order for increased medication. Face of a nurse, bland as a sheep, peering in. Walker's finger jabbing the air, sending her away.

Walker's finger, the yellowing pages in the dark study again, words flipping past.

A ring of doctors standing in a half-circle outside Snow's closed door, grim faces, discussing options, none of them good.

Walker's hand filling a coffee cup, spilling a little, the vision black-ringed with fatigue.

In his narrow room, the boy, disintegrating by whole orders of magnitude, colorless, death perched at his shoulder like an ugly bird.

Walker's reflection in a bathroom mirror, chin lathered with shaving cream, fatigued. Hand trembling, slipping until blood seeps from the nick in his throat. Fingertips roll the blood, examining it.

Monitors: barely a twitch of activity on the long electronic line. The boy slipping further, disappearing into the depths of his bed like a small boat between the waves.

Walker's point of view coming back into the narrow room. The door closing behind him.

Opening a canvas bag.

Taking out the book.

Seeing it, Mike struggled to draw back from the vision but the chain of events fastened around him, binding him tight. He stared in helpless paralysis as Walker's hands opened the book to the spot he'd marked.

The words like grave-dirt in his mouth.

Monitor needles jumping, then falling flat. Code alarms screaming. On the bed, the boy's body twitching once and falling still. Smell of burning hair, the shriek of butchered animals from deep within the earth. Heavy thumping vibrations in the floor beneath his feet giving way to—

Walker's point of view, looking down.

The floor opening up, a hole gaping under his feet, and through it, Walker looked down at the thing crawling out of this dark crack in the world, dragging itself into view. Something ageless, something from before man's primacy, neither God nor devil but some red, flayed-looking creature with gelid pools for eyes. Its head jerking toward Walker's point of view, jaws snapping open and shut with what was not—could not be—any human language.

Walker, turning, looking deeper into the hole to see how the chasm teemed with others just like the thing that had climbed out. The gap seemed to be crawling with them, thousands of inhuman prisoners like the one he'd just released.

Slapping the book shut.

Looking up again at the boy on the bed, little Frank Snow's eyes opening.

The boy pulling the breathing tube from his mouth.

Raising his head to look at Walker.

Lips moving to form words.

"Thank you."

Walker screaming, backing up, falling prostrate before the unfathomable enormity of his error—

Mike jolted backward, the book flinging him sideways into a brick wall, where painful awareness shot through him. Vision instantly clearing, he looked around.

He was in the hospital operators' office, the book open, the microphone switched on in front of him.

He had been reading from the page.

## 46

When the PA speaker started crackling, the voice reading, Jolie looked up from the map.

*Mike? What . . . ?*

The note she'd found here had told her to stay put in this chair and no matter what was asked, not to speak except for that single sentence, "Look at the camera." At first Jolie thought Snow was just using her to torment Sarah. *See? Here I am, in the middle of all this, getting reamed six ways to Sunday by your husband. Crazy, huh?*

But Mike had flat-out refused to do that. It had been his idea to take a close-up picture of the porno magazine couple instead, one where you couldn't see their faces. *It probably won't work,* Mike had said, *but that's all I'm doing. Freak out all you want, Jo, I'm not doing it. I'll find another way out for my family.*

And in the end, all that chivalry hadn't mattered for shit. When Jolie saw Calhoun grab the kid off the nurses' station counter, she realized all she and Mike had done was create a distraction. Whether the image in the picture was clear or not, they'd ended up doing Snow's bidding anyway.

She'd been about ready to get up and run when she saw the map. Snow had left it for her under the chair, the hand-drawn blueprint on the Bible page that had brought her up here in the first place, like some mocking reward for doing what was asked.

She'd looked at it, unable to shake the nagging suspicion that she'd missed something the first time she'd seen it. The exits were all here, the hallways and staircases, leading down to the ground floor.

Then Mike's voice started rattling through the PA. The language he spoke was not even close to English. Before this moment, Jolie never would have guessed that Mike knew any other language at all. He sounded stiff and atonal, like a man talking in his sleep, but despite everything, she recognized his voice at once.

The bizarre, creepy words made her stomach go into somersaults and barrel rolls. Involuntarily, her eyes went back to the map, and she thought about the underground tunnel, seeing it there for the first time, right in front of her nose—

Then: the gunshot.

## 47

To Sarah's eye, Mike's voice on the overhead speaker had an instantaneous effect on Snow. Three syllables in, he was sitting up. Within five seconds he was on his feet, opening and closing his fists, working the circulation into his hands. Two bright streams of fresh blood leaked from both nostrils simultaneously.

Calhoun, still holding Eli and the gun, took a step back. "What's going on?" he shouted. "What the fuck is he saying?"

*This is it,* Sarah thought. *This is why Snow lured all of us together, for this very moment—*

The floor jumped beneath their feet. Fresh smoke came gushing up from the hole in the room, along with all the noises of the hospital, streaming pipes and buzzing wires and the metallic grind of elevator cables thrashing into motion. Amid it all, Sarah saw Snow holding his arms up, drawing the chain of the handcuffs tight between his wrists. He seemed to bask in the moment, rising to his full height. Blood streamed from his eyes, ears, nose, but none of it appeared to affect him. If anything it bespoke some savage new virility, ascendancy to godhead. Beneath his shaved hairline Snow's cranial vault illuminated vividly from within like a candled egg, and inside it she was sure she glimpsed something, the outline of another head that was so far from human she couldn't believe it could be part of this same universe.

Hands still bound, the thing that had been Snow reached for Eli.

"*Here!*" Calhoun made a shrill gobbling sound, a combination of laughter and tears. "*Take him!*"

The smoke was getting thicker by the second. Sarah grabbed the gun, jerked it from the security guard's shock-limp hand. Enclosed in Snow's handcuffed arms, her son awoke with a scream.

*Do this right. You may only get one shot.*

Sarah pointed the pistol upward and squeezed the trigger.

In the tiny room the report was deafening, like a bomb. Mike's voice disappeared behind it. Up above, the PA speaker that she'd just put a bullet through dangled halfway off the wall on a braid of wires. Now it just spluttered with an incoherent beehive drone.

As soon as Mike's voice stopped, the thing inside Snow cringed forward, instantly weakened. Half its color had already slid away toward a kind of pasty pallor and the foreign object glowing within Snow's skull faded beneath the gray smoothness of the man's own skin and hair. Eli slid from his arms to the floor and ran back to Sarah, still screaming.

*"Please, Mommy, stop it, stop it! Please!"*

Snow's mouth dropped open. "You bitch. I made you a good deal. What have you done?"

"This," she said, pointing the gun at him, and pulled the trigger.

## 48

**Mike slammed his shoulder** against the door of the hospital operators' office and felt the latch snap. He'd hit it with everything he had and a little extra, something on loan from God. Leaning back, he drove his foot hard below the knob. The door flew open, crashed against the wall. He was down on the main floor, not far from the ER entrance.

*The stairs. Now.*

His feet took flight before he knew what was happening, propelling him through the hall to the stairwell. Fatigue felt a long way off, a luxury he might never have again. At the moment he could've gone on forever, certainly a few flights of steps weren't going to stop him, not now.

Four floors up, he ran into Jolie coming the other direction. Her hair and clothes were smoldering visibly, reeking of soot, her eyes frenzied and bloodshot. "Mike—"

"Are they up there?"

"What?"

"Sarah and Eli, are they still up there?"

"I couldn't see."

"Keep going."

She blinked, but didn't move. "Maybe . . . I can go back with you and—"

Mike shook his head. "Go. Get help." He moved past her, up the final flight of stairs, and out the door into Peds. He was standing at the far end of the corridor, where the air was still comparatively clear. Orienting himself to the layout of the hall, Mike looked in the other direction, into the rubbery black burning smell, eyes and nose already watering. He'd been through this once before and knew what it would be like that way, back where they'd taken Frank Snow the first time.

"Sarah!"

He turned and ran into the smoke. Being prepared for how bad it was didn't make it any better. Within seconds his vision was gone in a stinging wash of tears, black tar clogging his throat. He dropped to his hands and knees and crawled forward.

"Sarah! Eli!" He wanted his voice to be louder but even he could barely hear it. From up ahead, the chugging clank of heavy machinery grew louder, like chains being dragged and slapped across piles of sheet metal. It was as if something inside the hospital's infrastructure had broken free and was running faster and faster, cogs and pulleys ripping themselves to pieces.

Mike gripped the wall and kept going, the smoke's thickness a physical presence around him, filtering into his thoughts.

*How do you know they're even here?*

*I don't.*

*Go on back. It's all right, Lover Boy. They're safe. They're—*

Mike brought his hand to his mouth and bit his knuckle hard until the pain shot up his arm. It cut through the murk of his mind long enough for him to edge a few yards farther. Things were worse up ahead, no question. Blind and effectively deaf from the clatter of noise, he put one hand out for guidance and felt the floor shaking.

*Die,* the voice chattered, *you'll die up here, Lover Boy, alone and lost—*

Two choices: stop or keep going.

*They're not even here, they're downstairs already looking for you. You're on a fool's errand.*

Mike told the voice he'd go another ten paces and stop, knowing he wouldn't. He'd crawl every foot of this hall until he dropped, and the chattering voice in his head, the voice of the smoke, knew it, too. It had started chanting along with the beat of his heart.

*Quit. Quit. Quit.*

He put his other arm out, leaned on it and felt the unsteadiness of lactic acid buildup tremble through his muscles, the feeling of an exhausted swimmer who realizes that his arms and legs are overcooked pasta and he's going to drown. The adrenaline he'd felt earlier was gone. For the first time since he entered the smoke he felt scared, truly scared, that he wouldn't have control of himself, body or mind, anymore than he did in the operators' office. His determination to find his wife and child wouldn't matter one iota after that, because the thing in the hospital, the thing inside the smoke, would be calling the shots.

*How much time do I have left? Two minutes? Less?*

His palm skated forward, dropping him onto his face, and all at once he knew his time was up. His half-blind eyes rose up to the crayon drawings on the walls, the cancer kids, terminal but still doggedly manipulating their Crayolas, and he understood them in a way he never had before. They were monuments to the absolute indifference of the universe, an unfair place where the innocent suffered and everyone's best efforts didn't make a germ of difference, because what was ultimately meant to happen was ultimately going to happen.

A cold horror sprawled across his heart as he glimpsed his future without Sarah and Eli, the empty house, the scattered toys, clothes bagged, never to be worn again, a life he couldn't bear to look at, even obliquely.

The walls. The hallway. The smoke. Of the countless moments he'd spent, squandered, and savored with his wife and son, this was the one that counted. Everything else vanished in the light of that revelation and Mike fell in love with them all over again, with a fierceness that startled him into a species of out-of-body strength.

He put his hand out until the tips of his fingers felt something on the floor in front of him. Smooth skin, fabric, a sleeve or pant leg, he couldn't tell. Grasping it, he pulled closer until he saw Sarah's face through the smoke, eyes closed, coming into focus. She had curled herself around Eli's small body, neither of them moving in the black depths.

"Hey," Mike croaked, kneeling and lifting her up. "It's me."

She coughed, glassine eyes opening, runny with tears. "Mike?" It was barely a whisper. "You're here?"

"Come on."

"Can't walk. Can't . . . breathe." A flicker of realization in her eyes: "*Eli*—"

"I've got him." Mike lifted the boy in one arm, his left. He'd need his right for Sarah.

*Who are you kidding? You don't have the strength for this. You can hardly move yourself.*

With Eli on his shoulder, he put his back to the wall and hooked his hand as low as possible around Sarah's hips. The trick was going to be resisting the impulse to rely on his back. If it went out when he tried to lift, he doubted any of them would get another chance.

He took a deep breath and pushed as hard as he could. His legs were tired from running through the hospital all night, but they were still strong compared to the rest of him. Levering his body upward with the wall behind him, he stood erect with Eli under one arm and Sarah the other. For one bad moment he teetered, almost falling, then steadied and started lumbering back up the hall.

Somewhere in the smoke he found the strength to keep going.

**49.**

"Mike?"

Hands, shaking him. Not Sarah, too forceful for her. Layers of scalding blackness lifted from his vision and he saw Dr. Walker in front of him.

"Where's . . . ?" he started to ask, but his larynx wasn't up to the task and he started coughing up what felt like white-hot razor blades from the back of his throat into the delicate webbing of his vocal cords.

"Easy," Walker said. "Your wife and son are all right. You got them out."

Mike realized he was on his back and pushed himself up on his elbows. "Where . . . ?"

"Still upstairs. Put this on." Walker put an oxygen mask over Mike's nose and mouth. "Just breathe in and out. Try not to cough if you can help it."

Mike breathed in dry air until the pain in his throat started to fade. As he breathed he watched Walker's eyes, the doctor gazing back at him, finally removing the mask.

Mike felt his anger rise, the evening's frustration building inside him now that he had Walker as a focal point. He stopped himself, forced the irritation down. The doctor had probably just saved his life. "I know about you and Snow."

Walker didn't move. Then he understood. "The book."

"Why did you bring him back here?"

"To get rid of what I put inside him," Walker said. "I tried tonight—I tried twice. Failed both times. It wasn't going to work." He tilted his head to the side. "She pulled a gun on him."

Turning his head, Mike saw Sarah sitting against the wall with Eli in her arms, both of them with their eyes closed. Jolie stood behind them, apart. Mike reached over and squeezed his wife's hand.

Her eyes opened, recognized him. It might've been a smile.

"You shot the bastard?" Jolie asked, sounding reluctantly impressed.

Sarah turned her head toward Jolie, nodded warily.

"Aim for his balls?"

"A little higher."

"Probably just as well." After a moment, Jolie turned to Walker. "The way I see it, the tunnel's our only chance. It's on the map, six floors straight down."

"That's Snow's map," Walker said.

Jolie pointed at the thick black smoke crowding down from the other end of the hall. "You have any better suggestions?"

"She's right," Sarah managed. "Let's take the stairs."

Jolie looked at her for a moment without speaking. Then they went through, she and Walker first followed by Sarah and Eli, with Mike in back, clutching the railing for support. Up in front of him, he saw the boy lift his head from Sarah's shoulders, a purple lump above his eye.

"Daddy?"

"Hey, big guy." Mike smiled for the first time in what felt like forever. "Look who it is."

"I missed you so much."

"Missed you, too."

"Are we gonna be okay?"

"Honey, we are walking out of here."

"Right now?"

"Right now."

But the stairs took a long time. At the bottom of the lowest flight, Walker took them through an open set of double doors, following the hallway down a corrugated metal ramp. The air was humid and smelled like mildewed linen, rotten paper, and old exhaust. They had reached the maintenance hall, passing rows of broken wheelchairs that would never be repaired, and an entire wall of old folders and paperwork that had been crammed into bare shelves, clear to the dead light fixtures above.

"Watch your step." Walker had stopped next to a giant electric substation, where a bundle of cables rose up and bypassed the beginning of an out-landishly large water main. Next to the water main was one final door, a green steel thing on rusty hinges, already propped open.

Standing with his wife and son, Mike peered through the doorway and into the tunnel. It was even longer than he'd expected, stretching straight ahead and angling slightly downward for what he guessed was two hundred yards before it came bending back up, so that anything beyond that was not visible. He didn't like that. He liked it even less than the stench of stagnant, bacteria-smelling water breathing out from deep inside, as if they were stand-ing in the gullet of a dying giant and looking down into its contaminated lungs. Across the ceiling, a single pipe the color of plumber's caulk and the width of a good-sized oak tree ran down into the tunnel's depths.

He touched Sarah's hand. "Where did you hit Snow when you shot him?"

"In the chest."

"Then what happened?"

"He fell down."

"Dead?"

She just looked at him.

"I wasn't there," Mike said, and he could already tell they were sharing a thought, probably the same one running through Jolie's mind and Walker's as well. *What if he's still alive? What if the other end is locked?*

Water dripped and oozed intermittently from the ceiling pipe, and the concrete floor beneath them was visibly damp. Far away Mike heard a soft pattering sound.

"It looks like about a quarter-mile from here to the far end," Jolie's voice said from up ahead, echoing down the length of the tunnel. "The old research facility is down at the other side."

Mike linked hands with Sarah and Eli. Immediately to his left, he saw three bicycles leaned against the wall, old Schwinns from another era, the ones the maintenance crews had left there in the event they had to venture to the other end.

There was a sharp clang behind them.

Up ahead, Walker stopped and spun back in the direction they'd come. The green metal door they'd just passed through was now closed.

The stillness of the moment shattered around them, its components scattering everywhere. Mike heard noises growing louder up the tunnel, rusty scratching sounds, like rats scrambling down a metal pipe. It seemed to be coming from overhead. He felt a clammy tide of panic spill over him, tugging him back in its wake.

He looked up.

Snow was clinging to the ceiling of the tunnel above them. His head hung upside down, swinging and bobbing like a toy on a broken spring, jaws snapping open and shut as he tensed to launch at them. The mask of humanity, once convincing enough, now felt like something projected on him by a low-watt projector bulb, an illusion that would vanish with the flick of a switch, leaving only some unimaginably black armature of horror. Mike thought of what the book had shown him—the book he'd come to realize had been the thing's portal for entering this world.

*If he's not human, what is he? What is it?*

Yet he knew. Perhaps not a name, but the name would be the least of it. From outside our world, Dr. Walker had brought forth something both playful and toxic—playful until it started losing, the way it had up on the sixth floor. After that its anger would be as lethal as it was limitless.

A sudden unsteadiness in the floor itself plunged Mike sideways and pitched him facedown on the concrete. Crawling backward, he felt the foot of an elephant step on his back, slamming his chest to the ground hard enough to crack his ribs against his sternum. Hot salt trickled through his nose and mouth, warping his vision.

A voice from above said: "They're mine."

As he raised his head, Mike realized he was still looking at Snow dangling from the pipe above him. Who was on his back?

Then some animal part of him realized it, had maybe already realized it, even before he saw Snow was still hanging from the pipe.

*Calhoun.*

Twisting around as far as he could, Mike saw Walker, Sarah, and Eli hovering in his peripheral vision. They were staring at the thing that stood between his shoulder blades. To Mike, their eyes looked uniformly whited-out with an expression of surprise so broad and bold it was almost comical.

Snow sprung from the ceiling pipe, shooting toward him, and Mike felt the weight of the thing on his back vanish as quickly as it had appeared. All five of his senses died without a flicker. From behind him he heard a crash followed by a muffled, meaty slam. There was a hoarse scream and then a gasp.

Pause . . .

And his vision came back in screens of phosphorescent dots.

Sarah, Eli, Walker, and Jolie were gone.

It hurt to look higher but he did. Calhoun dangled a foot off the ground, impaled to the wall of the tunnel on a long steel spear. His face was a portrait of crucified insanity, a half-mad messiah who had died with only a passing knowledge of the circumstances that had ultimately brought him low. Almost before Mike's eyes, the first shadows of familiarity began seeping back into Calhoun's face as the last of his life drained out. The dark scarlet puddle beneath his feet spread wider, reaching out in all directions to encompass the floor.

Calhoun raised his head. Some final ember of lucidity glittered in his eyes, as if he'd just remembered a name or some detail that had escaped him until now. He gazed at Mike and his lips moved briefly, webbed by blood.

"Mike . . ." He hesitated and his head slumped forward, his voice ground down to less than a whisper. Mike wouldn't have heard it if he hadn't been so close. "Tunnel . . . locked . . . at the other end—" A bubble of blood swelled on his lips and burst. "I did it . . . I'm s-sorry—"

"So we're trapped?"

Calhoun shook his head, held out one hand. It seemed to require all he had. Mike watched as the security guard opened his fingers, giving him the key ring, pointing at the big bronze key—the ER door upstairs.

"What happened to Sarah and Eli?"

Calhoun shook his head, mouthing one word.

*Snow.*

## 50

"Give me the boy."

Sarah turned with Eli in her arms. With Dr. Walker out of the picture, she had no protector, no weapon, no shield except her own body. After everything that had transpired throughout the hospital, upstairs and downstairs, in the dark and in the light, it had boiled down to this.

What happened to Walker had been a bad surprise, perhaps the worst yet. Somehow, despite everything, Sarah had expected him to come through for them in the end. But she had never seen someone rise up so recklessly, or go down so fast.

When Snow had made his move on Calhoun a few moments earlier, Walker had hustled her and Eli up the tunnel, despite her protestations of leaving Mike behind. They hadn't gotten far at all before Snow had caught up to them, devouring the expanse like a harsh and vengeful wind. There *was* something of the forces of nature in him now, Sarah was sure of it, nature's dark side, at least, a cruelty he'd absorbed from less than human influences. It had all happened so rapidly—and in retrospect, so inevitably.

When the sound of his laughter drew closer and Walker had gone stock-still, it had been with the grim, self-defeating fatalism of a man who knew he stood no chance but could not stop himself. He'd propelled himself bodily at Snow's chest, and Snow's red right hand had snapped out hooklike, faster than Sarah could see; almost casually, in a parody of motion, Walker dropped to a heap, where he now lay motionless, unresponsive, barely breathing.

"Thought you were smart shooting me, didn't you?" Snow asked Sarah now, stepping over Walker's body, pointing to the clotted hole in his prison jumpsuit. "You should have held up your half of the deal." Irrational events were occurring now, phenomena for which she had no words. Inside the semitransparent globe of Snow's skull, under the stubble of his hair, something gelatinous shone and pulsed, more clearly this time, seeming to throb in time with his words. It made his voice sound different. "Not that it matters. I'm finished with this body."

He brought out a fire ax that Sarah hadn't seen until now, the one Calhoun had been holding before Snow had slammed him into the side of the tunnel. When she tried to move backward, all she felt were walls coming together to form a corner crowding against her back.

*If Eli can run, if he can somehow get away—*

"The boy," Snow said, seeming to read her thoughts. "If he wants, he can watch me do my business with you." He turned to Eli. "What do think, boy meat? Want a little reminder of what Mommy's insides look like?"

Eli opened his mouth but no scream came—nothing came. He was an empty vessel, pushed far beyond his limits. His eyes were hollow cups in his skull.

"Hmm." Snow smiled. "I think you're going to enjoy this. Maybe not right away, but definitely—"

Something slammed into his head, flinging him sideways into the side of the tunnel. The ax left his hands, clattering to the floor. As he fell, Sarah found herself staring at the woman behind him holding a length of plastic pipe, hair hanging in her face.

"Jolie?"

Jolie looked at her. "This time go for his balls."

She started to say more and Snow's hand rammed up to seize her throat. Sarah saw Jolie's eyes flash to hers, a split second of recognition arcing like some fugitive moment of telepathy between them, the last darting sparks of life looking for a place to land. It ended when Snow wrenched Jolie's neck with a single twisting snap. With that snap, everything vital—color, beauty, adrenaline, life—dropped in a single lump from Jolie's face. Snow opened his hand and her body fell to the floor.

Sarah's muscles sprung up of their own volition. She jumped to her feet and took Eli's hand, getting ready to start running for the far end of the tunnel. Off to the side, she saw Snow looking for where the ax had been.

But the ax was gone.

She turned, thinking automatically that there'd been a miracle, that the doctor had regained consciousness to save them all. But it wasn't Walker.

It was her husband.

It was Mike.

**51.**

**Seeing Snow from the back,** Mike had felt the handle of the ax on the floor practically flying into his grip like a natural extension of his arm, trembling from shaft to blade with the slamming thump of his heart. All fear and pain disappeared. His thoughts, moments earlier a jumbled scrawl, became a single broad brushstroke across an otherwise blank canvas.

He watched Snow, caught off-guard, turning with his whole body, a shuffling, graceless roundelay. In one smooth movement, knowing exactly what was required, he raised the ax and swung it down with all his strength.

There was a dull, bone-rending chop from deep inside Snow's upper musculature. He arched forward, an incoherent shriek, sprawling to the floor with the ax lodged deep within the muscles of his back. For a split second Mike thought he felt the entire hospital tremble, its enormous, multichambered heart splintered at the core by the blow he'd dealt, like a pond with a crack in the center, spreading outward. In the mirror of his own mind, he imagined he glimpsed a hole in the darkness big enough for them to crawl through, a hole the size of Frank Snow's body.

Mike put his arms around Sarah and Eli. "You're all right?"

"Eli and I are." Sarah lowered her eyes and Mike saw Jolie's body for the first time, fallen into shadow, motionless. "Jolie . . . She put herself in harm's way for us."

"What about Walker?" Mike reached for him and felt the doctor forcing himself to his feet, cringing away from Mike's attempts to help him up. Something had silenced him, an intolerable lapse of personal responsibility that could not be countenanced in the face of the man's formidable ego. Maybe it was the simple fact that his inability to stop Snow had not yet cost him his life. Whatever the case, Mike could feel shame radiating off the man's skin like fever.

He glanced back up at Sarah. "Hold Eli," he said. "Let's go."

Sarah glanced deeper into the tunnel. "Back that way?"

"No." Mike shook his head. "It's locked at the other end."

Walker spoke quietly. "How do you know?"

"Calhoun."

"Is he . . . ?"

Mike nodded. "We have to go back."

"How are we going to get out?"

Mike held up the security guard's keys.

## 52

At the entrance to the tunnel, where the green doors gave way to the rest of the hospital, Walker spoke again.

"Snow's weak," he said, "but he'll be back. He needs your son now more than ever."

Mike felt every part of his body fall heavy and still, as if his insides had been replaced with a poured plaster cast of themselves. "With the ax still in him?"

Walker's expression hadn't changed. "Let me go back and try to find him. At least I can create some kind of diversion so you and your family can run for the exit."

Mike stopped and thought about it. "There might be another way."

"Even weakened, you won't be able to kill what's inside of him."

"We'll see."

Walker looked at him. "What are you thinking?"

"I'll need your help," Mike said.

They went back up, heading through the door to MRI. Mike crossed the suite to the outer console, past the desk. The red button outside the scan room was confined in a yellow square and shielded by a hinged piece of thick plastic. The sign beneath the button said:

EMERGENCY SWITCH
Operation of this switch will deenergize the magnet.
WARNING!
Energizing the magnet is a long and very costly process.

Mike read these words over, as he had a hundred times before, then looked back at Walker, Sarah, and Eli. The four of them were right in front of the outer console, less than twenty feet from where the man with the serpent tattoo had been handcuffed in his stretcher the first time he had laid eyes on him, six hours and a million years ago.

"Come over here," Mike said. "We'll need to stay down."

"Mike?" Sarah blinked at him. "What are you doing?"

But Dr. Walker was nodding. "I think I know what to do," he said. "It's all right."

"Listen—"

"You have to trust me. I can do what's required. I still have that ability." Walker's eyes darted to the red button on the wall. Then he seemed not to notice the rest of them at all. "You do, too, don't you?" he asked without turning around.

Without waiting for Mike's answer, the doctor walked to the doorway of the scan room, leaving the door open behind him. For a moment Mike saw Walker through the glass, standing in front of the magnet, his scorched and bloody lab coat hanging off him like the last remaining actor at the end of some modern adaptation of a Shakespearean tragedy.

Sarah's voice whispered, "Mike, what's he . . . ?"

"Shh." He reached down and found the shape of her hand. "Crawl down here under the table with me." He helped her and Eli out of the chair, guiding them along the floor beneath the table until his wife and child were braced against the wall. "Stay here. Whatever happens, don't move and don't make a sound."

Then, from across the room, he heard a shape coming in from the hallway, breathing raggedly. Mike sensed it hovering there, not moving.

"Hello, Frank," Walker's voice said.

Mike raised his head as much as he dared, unable now to avert his eyes. Coming here had cost him so much, almost everything, and he needed to see it finished.

He could see Snow looking into the scan room, wavering unsteadily with the hallway behind him, mouth slightly open, shoulders rising and falling with the exertion of his arrival. The handle of the ax still jutted upward from between his shoulder blades where Mike had planted it—it trembled a little with his breathing, like a wooden tail. Standing there, he looked more dead than alive, yet more dangerous than ever, kept upright solely by the twin life-support systems of his own rage and madness, and the inhuman thing that knotted them together at the rotten plexus of his being.

"Where . . . ?"

"Over here," Walker said.

"Not . . . you," Snow croaked. "The boy." He staggered around sideways and the handle of the ax whacked the doorway, the impact making him wince. From his hiding place behind the desk, Mike straightened up to follow his shambling progress toward the doorway of the scan room.

Through the glass, Mike could see Walker waiting in the room, sitting on the table where Snow had gotten his scan. The neurologist sat with one leg crossed over the other and his hands folded on his lap. It was the quintessential physician's pose, the body language of a man prepared to deliver a sizable slice of life-changing news, good, bad, or uncertain.

"Come in here," Walker said. "I want to talk to you."

"About . . . what?"

"Oh, there are a few things." The doctor spread his hands. "For example, do you really know who you are?"

"Doesn't matter. It's over. You lost."

Walker's glance was sympathetic, almost pitying. "Look at you, Frank. You can hardly stand upright."

"Not . . . for long. I'm taking the boy's body. It's young . . . strong. *Where is he?*"

"I don't know."

"Lying!"

"Am I?" Walker asked mildly. "At this point, why bother?" He patted the table next to him. "Come on, Frank. Let's talk. You'll find we have more in common than you think."

## 53

**Frank Snow didn't move.** Dr. Walker remained exactly where he was, a study in patience. With minutes left to live, he gave no thought to neurology or any facet of medicine that had consumed so much of life until now. For the first time in what felt like decades, Tanglewood Memorial Hospital was nowhere near his mind; it was like a dream to him now, something that had happened to another man entirely.

He was thinking about a nurse named Lana.

She and Walker had dated during his first year of residency, and things had gotten serious very quickly. She'd gotten pregnant that fall. At twenty-nine, Walker had harbored no delusions of blundering into fatherhood. His suggestion at the time was that Lana get an abortion, an idea that she responded to by quitting the hospital not long afterward, returning home to her parents' house in Dayton, Ohio, to have the child and raise it without him. It was the last he'd heard from her for three years, until Lana, whose last name had been Snow, had called and said that she was coming back through Pennsylvania on her way to New York, and would Walker like to meet his young son?

They had met, ultimately, in the Peds ICU, after the crash.

Walker had never told anyone that the boy in the corner room was his illegitimate son. Yet at the same time, he couldn't quite believe no one had questioned the bond that had formed so blatantly between himself and Frank Snow. Apparently, such gross outward displays of personal commitment were par for the course for residents. The nurses all thought he was sweet; his attendings thought he was ridiculous and soft, too much of an idealist.

But Walker had not been able to let his son slip away.

"Frank?" Walker said, looking down the length of the flashlight beam. "Are you still out there?"

"What . . . do you . . . want?"

"The same thing I wanted before," Walker said. "To tell you what you really are."

"You know what I am. This *is* . . . what I am."

"Before all that."

Snow nearly entered the room now, not comprehending. "What are you talking about?"

"You're my son."

Snow stopped.

"Come on. It's not only possible, it's true."

The impending significance of this revelation struck a discordant note in Snow's face, and his expression burst wide open in a wasp's nest of bitterness and fury.

"You *know* it's true." Walker's voice was almost tender.

"You know where I came from," he shouted. "I am no one's son!"

Snow charged inside. From Walker's vantage point, he barely glimpsed Mike pull himself up on his haunches beside the desk, and peer in through the glass. Walker knew the magnetic field of the scanner, what they called the Gauss line, extended in a six-foot circle from the bore. Snow was just entering that radius when a great invisible hand seemed to grab hold of the steel-bladed ax imbedded in his back, spinning him around like a top and yanking him off his feet, pulling him toward the center of the magnet.

"Mike!" Walker shouted. *"Now!"*

## 54

**On the other side,** Mike leaped up, slammed the door of the room behind Snow, and hit the red button with the palm of his right hand.

For the first second or two, nothing happened.

Through the tinted glass he could see Snow pinned to the side of the magnet by the ax blade, his limbs writhing and wriggling like a beetle in a child's insect collection. Then the entire room began to rumble like a freight train as the pressure vessel inside the magnet's plastic casing strained against the abrupt bulge of gas expanding within it. Titanium bolts popped off, whistling as they streaked across the room like a hail of bullets, smacking off the walls. From above there was a sharp pang as the vent pipe burst.

Snow jolted up, staring out at Mike in surprise.

The vessel exploded.

The room went white as a frozen cloud of helium fog spilled through it, instantly crystallizing the window in a thick layer of frost. Mike couldn't see anything. Reflexively, not even aware that he was doing so, he drew closer to the glass, squinting to make out what was happening inside.

A gray claw smacked the glass in front of his face and he jerked back.

Through the streak of clarity that the claw had slashed across the frosty glass, he could see Snow in his truest undeveloped form, the rawness that had been incubating inside. He saw it for a fraction of a second, but that fraction was enough to last an entire lifetime.

Snow was still in the prison jumpsuit, but the fabric had split open on the sides to allow for a lashing outburst of flailing roachlike limbs. They looked lethal, but they also looked queerly vulnerable, comprised of soft tissue that had never been intended for exposure to outside elements. Staring at them

Mike felt himself going a little mad, his brain stretched beyond its capacity for reason, like waking up in the glare of a screaming blue sun.

If hell was real, this thing had almost surely come from there.

One of the limbs was struggling blindly to pluck the ax from its back, which now resembled more of a carapace than any sort of human skin. Sticky translucent fluid dripped from its pale inner membrane. Another limb fumbled at the door latch. Through the fog Mike saw how Snow's spine had elongated and doubled over on itself, arching like an inchworm's, his long alligator head twisting and snapping from the warped infrastructure of his shoulders. He grinned at Mike, yellow-eyed, cackling, the sickening fullness of his exposed body telescoping inward.

Mike saw it coming, and in retrospect he thought Walker must have, too. One of the snapping claws shot forward. It fastened onto Walker's throat, compressing the wrinkled wattles beneath the doctor's chin, just above the collar of his shirt. At the same time Mike saw Snow's movement stiffening, losing all fluidity. Frost hardened over the grin, over the gleaming gray slug-flesh, filming the eyeballs, turning them to globes of isinglass.

The claw snapped shut.

Blood spurted brightly from Walker's severed throat, piping in quarts down over the buglike pincer. It ran up the long extension of the arm, but by the time it reached what was left of Snow's body, the thing lay motionless on the floor. Clouds of wet steam rose from the hardened cracks of half-solidified armor, and it didn't move again.

The last thing Mike saw before he turned away was Dr. Walker's body as it fell forward, into the grip of the thing's arm.

That was how Mike left them, as he turned to find his own family, huddled beneath the table.

# 55.

Little by little Mike herded them toward the door. Lifting Sarah in one arm and Eli in the other, he carried them up the stairs. The keys were in his hand. He knew the world he'd find outside would be the one he'd known, the place that he and his family called home.

For the first time in three years Mike Hughes left Tanglewood Memorial Hospital without punching the time clock.

His shift was over.

Calhoun's key turned in the lock without resistance. Outside, the night sky was clear enough that he could count the stars. After helping his wife and son over the steps, Mike looked up and saw the parking lots and the woods beyond it.

*That's our lives out there,* he thought, a little deranged. The notion inspired a simultaneous outburst of hope and open-ended apprehension.

"Mike?" Sarah looked at him weakly. "Can we get out of here?"

"Right now." And he remembered the car keys, downstairs with the rest of the belongings.

"It's all right." She opened her hand, revealing the key ring she had left down in MRI, the keys that had brought her back the first time. "I've got them."

"That's good then."

By the time they got to the car, he thought the boy had fallen asleep, but Eli was awake and watching them.

Mike kissed his cheek. A dazed vision of the future wafted into his mind, the three of them living somewhere else, perhaps up north. Mike would work strict daylight hours at an outpatient facility. There would be no midnight shift, no three a.m. calls, no empty hallways, no half-empty beds. He would be home every night for dinner. When Eli got older he'd help him with his homework. He would take him to swim lessons and go trick-or-treating on Halloween. If Eli asked questions about what had happened on this night, Mike would do his best to answer them, but he would never bring the subject up himself. He and Sarah would not speak of it, either, not if they could help it.

He put Eli into his car seat and strapped him in. Sarah climbed in back next to the boy. Things were not going to be easy for any of them, not for a long time, perhaps ever again. There would be sleepless nights, bad dreams, and long silences. But in his mind he was already driving them north, away from Pennsylvania, toward the broad expanse of New England, an area whose history and durability might give some context to what had happened to them tonight, or at least allow them to live with it.

"What time is it?" Sarah asked.

He started the car. "Just after two."

"It feels later."

"Four hours till daylight."

He pulled out of the parking spot. From behind he felt Sarah's hand reaching up between the seats to touch his shoulder. Her fingers were tentative but her voice was as strong as he remembered it ever being.

"It's all right," she said. "We'll be all right, Mike."

"Sarah," and suddenly there were tears in his eyes, as the awfulness of what had happened began settling inside him with all its unbearable weight. "I'm so sorry. This is all my fault."

"No," she said, and he heard that she was crying, too, softly. "I love you. Do you love me?"

"Yes. God, yes."

"You know what I was thinking as Eli and I were lost in the smoke upstairs, right before you came back? I was thinking how lucky I was, how blessed, because I knew it was going to be okay. Do you see that?"

Mike nodded. He did see that, but she had it turned around. He was the fortunate one, and he knew it. For whatever reason he had been worried about saving his wife and child, when in reality, of course, his wife and child had saved him. By the time the sun rose they'd be at another hospital, and things would be better.

He drove across the employee lot to where he'd parked his own car, hours before.

"Mike, what . . . ?"

"It's all right." He got out, Sarah watching as he stepped from the Outback and walked to his car, reached into the glove compartment, and brought out a black velvet box he'd left there. Without a word he got back into the driver's seat, turned around, and put the box in her hand.

Sarah opened it. The bracelet shone in the half-light, reflected in her eyes.
Its inscription: SARAH—FOREVER—MIKE.

"It's beautiful." She looked at him. "Why?"

"No reason."

She looked back up at him, tears in her eyes.

Mike Hughes put their car in gear and drove his family home.

Dave Kellogg thought: *It's dead.*

He nudged the rat with the tip of his work boot, keeping his flashlight pointed at it. It was the third one he'd found since entering the hospital via the broken window in the ER waiting room. What had killed them all? Why were they down here in the first place? He was beginning to think Tanglewood hadn't been much of a health-care facility even when it still had patients in it, six months earlier. No wonder the place had gone out of business.

Dave had been in a lot of old hospitals; it was his thing. His uncle Walt ran a salvage business outside of Harrisburg, and there was big money to be had in some of these old facilities, if you got there before the other scavengers did. Old equipment, tools, furniture, all of those things were good, but Dave knew if you could get to the pipes down in radiology, you'd struck the mother lode. And at twenty-six, Dave Kellogg was all about the mother lode.

He checked the photocopy of the plumbing schematic that a friend in the Lebanon County Assessor's Office had made for him, and studied the distance from here to the basement. Once he got there, it was simply a matter of locating the right pipes. The ones that ran from the water main to the darkroom were the ones he wanted. In a hospital as old as this one those pipes would be lined with an inch-thick residue from decades of developing solutions used in X-rays. To the untrained eye that runoff would present itself as unremarkable black grime, but when Mike boiled those pipes at his uncle's shop, he knew full well what he'd get: pound after pound of pure silver nitrate. Take that shit to auction and you'd walk away with some serious cheddar. Enough for a new car, better clothes, finer women, and the quality of life a guy like him deserved. Silver wasn't everything, but it was a hell of a start.

Following the map, he started down the stairs. They were covered in grit and his boots made soft crunching sounds as he descended. Once he found what he was looking for, he'd go up and get the sledgehammer and wrenches out in the truck. No sense in—

He stopped and cocked his head, listening. Down at the bottom of the stairs, on the other side of the door, he'd heard something rustling. If it was a rat, he thought, it was a damned big one.

*And if it wasn't a rat . . . ?*

A quick gray moth of fear fluttered over his skin and he shuddered, even as he hated himself for doing so. He knew what had happened here six months ago. Everybody did. That serial killer Frank Snow had gotten loose and killed a bunch of people down here, including cops, before he'd busted loose and escaped. Despite a massive manhunt, the police had never tracked him down. Dave's personal theory was that Snow was either dead or living somewhere in South America. He was no detective, but the odds of Snow poking up his head anywhere in the English-speaking world struck him as pretty damned thin.

And yet . . .

People said other things, too.

They talked about the hospital, and what had really gone down here that last awful night. Dave's uncle told him there'd been human sacrifices and worse. Unexplained weather patterns. Weird lights in the sky. The only people to survive were a family that had moved back to Maine immediately afterward. They hadn't talked to the media about what they'd seen.

Not that Dave Kellogg thought much about it before, but now he found himself wondering what would happen if Snow had never left the hospital. There were plenty of places down here to hide, empty tunnels and hallways where nobody would ever look. Snow could've been down here in the darkness right now, just behind the door. Waiting for somebody to wander down, poking around.

"Knock it off," he told himself, more harshly than he'd meant to. "Fifteen minutes down here and you're crying like a little girl."

Still, he really didn't want to go through that next door. What he wanted to do was to turn around and go back upstairs, go home, drink some beer, smoke some weed, and play some video games. If his uncle wanted that silver so badly, why then guess what, he could come down there himself and get it. Dave would even go with him—in broad daylight.

*Good plan,* a sour voice chided. *Maybe if you wait long enough, he'll go down and get it himself. And he'll KEEP it for himself, too, all that silver, just waiting for the right guy to come along and scoop it up. I guess that's not you, huh?*

Dave thought about it.

The voice would not be argued with.

The voice would not be reasoned with.

He opened the door.

His flashlight swept the darkness, picking out fallen chunks of drywall, the sagging walls oozing moisture. Turning right he found himself at the mouth of a long hallway. It was surprisingly warm down here in contrast to the night air. Just a moment earlier he'd been able to see his breath. Now he was actually sweating.

Something caught his eye.

Up ahead, thirty feet or so down the narrow corridor, he saw several partially exposed pipes sticking out of the wall.

"It's the mother lode, baby," he murmured, not feeling much better, speaking with more bravado than he actually felt. "You better believe it."

With the uneasy, rubbery sensation that he was not entirely in control of his legs, he walked down the hall to the pipes. For the first time since he'd broken in, he was aware of the largeness of the place around him, the vast silence of all this emptiness holding its breath. Squatting down, he aimed the flashlight into the pipe and looked inside. There was something glittering deep inside the pipe. It might have been liquid or solid, he wasn't sure, but from here it looked like—

"*Holy shit!*" he squeaked, jerking backward. The thing inside the pipe was moving toward him. He tried to step backward and his shoulder slammed into the wall. One foot angled crookedly across something behind him, twisting his leg, sending him spilling sideways toward that filthy floor. Dave's hands flew out to break his fall, and he had time to think that it must've been the biggest rat he'd ever seen in his life coming out of that pipe.

That did it.

"Screw you, buddy," he said to the pipe, standing up again and brushing off his pants. "I'll be back later or maybe I won't. But for tonight I'm out of here. This kid is gone."

His flashlight went out.

The blackness fell over him in a thick, impenetrable cloak. Dave's legs did a fast one-eighty and charged blindly in the direction of the stairs. He wasn't thinking about silver anymore, or what it could buy him. In the brilliant lucidity of his fright, the only thing he was thinking about was what had killed all the rats he'd found down here.

It was down here in the basement with him, whatever it was, closing in on him in the dark. His foot hooked over something sharp and he fell to the floor.

A thick slithery shape, terribly quick and muscular, squirmed past his bare forearm, moving up toward his head. Terror gripped him utterly then, and there was a faint, warm wetness as his bladder let go. Dave screamed, and even as he screamed, he could hear the slithering thing settling in next to him with a questing, insinuating presence that seemed intelligent somehow, knowing. It slid past his cheek and encircled his head, groping for the blood vessels in his neck. His veins and arteries, he realized, were what it wanted, a means of getting inside him.

At last he understood.

The thing in the dark did not want to *kill* him.

The thing in the dark did not want to *hurt* him.

The thing in the dark promised him all the silver he wanted.

Dave Kellogg opened his veins to receive the mother lode.

## About the Author

JOE SCHREIBER was born in Michigan but spent his formative years in Alaska, Wyoming, and Northern California. Until recently, he had never lived at the same address for longer than a year. Becoming a parent forced him to consider a career with a more reliable income, so he took a job as an MRI tech in Hershey, Pennsylvania, where he lives with his wife and their two children.